MIRROF

Jacques Von Kat

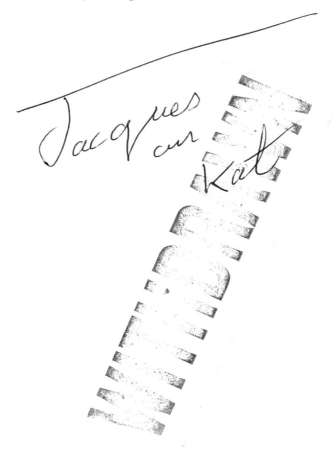

Broadthumb Publishing

Cover by: EC Editorial Cover Designs

For our parents.

&

In loving memory of Frankie, Wayne and Craig. Gone too soon.

CONTENTS

CHAPTER ONE

April 1984

I WATCHED THE WORLD and the townsfolk pass me by from the reflections in the shop windows. This part of town was my favourite place to people-watch in my hometown of Thorne, as the façade was made entirely from reflective glass. My second-favourite location was outside the library, though I didn't sit there often with it being opposite the police station. This spot was better, longer, and I could watch everyone via the store fronts until they vacated my line of sight.

I watched the world like this every day, though it rarely changed. The local family-run shops were dull and gloomy with their aluminium or wooden doors and faded lettering. Even the graffiti on the walls and shop shutters was black and white; the favourite line of the moment was "*Thatcher is a…*"

I couldn't repeat the last word.

The town's façade may have been dreary, but it was the inhabitants I was waiting to see. They brought colour to the world around me. Streaked hair, neon tracksuits, and khaki pants were the current styles. I'd never seen such an array of colours—some days it seemed people had stepped right off the catwalk. Folks around here followed the trends in magazines and *Top of the Pops*—now even men were wearing makeup. I didn't know what that was about; you'd never catch me in blue eyeshadow.

A group of screeching mothers strolled past, pushing their even louder screaming kids, no doubt making their way to playgroup or a coffee morning. A police car passed by resembling a giant jam sandwich, and I kept my head down 'til it was gone.

My preferred spot was a battered wooden bench covered by remnants of green paint and which had a concrete frame on either side. With all the jagged reminders of who had sat here before or who was boyfriend and girlfriend, it was apparent to me that everyone who had sat on this bench before me either had a pocketknife or a marker pen in their pocket. I'd yet to include my name; I'd never had a girlfriend, or even kissed a girl.

I scratched off a lone streak of green paint with my fingernail to reveal the rest of the brown slat underneath, then picked at the tiny flecks stuck under my nail. I liked to keep my hands clean, and not only my hands; my face was also scrubbed clean every morning. I couldn't see any excuse to be dirty if you had access to water—soap was a bonus. When I'd attended school, some kids were unkempt. I couldn't fathom why; they had to have had water at home, surely.

I looked back at the glass windows, and my pulse quickened as I spotted a suitable candidate. I examined the man's reflection as it sauntered by. He was of average height (around five foot nine), his brown hair was permed, and he had a moustache. The man walked with his hands tucked in his jean pockets, and he leaned slightly to the left. If he had moved his hands up to his belt loops and worn a Stetson, he could have passed for an extra from a Spaghetti Western. I nicknamed him "The Texan." I gave a name to everyone I followed. I had a nickname too: "The Mirror Man."

The man reminded me of a gunslinger, and the sight of him brought me back to this morning's conversation with my grandad during breakfast. He hadn't stopped talking about Marvin Gaye being shot since it had been reported in yesterday's paper. He liked his songs; I'd often catch him singing *I Heard It Through the Grapevine.* I would laugh when he couldn't hit the notes—no one in our family was a particularly good singer, though we all loved music.

Grandad couldn't understand what had happened to Mr Gaye. He'd only been forty-five—'No age at all.' His words, not mine. He said guns in America were meant to be for protection, not shooting like you were in the Wild West. I told him I was glad we didn't have them where we lived.

Mum snapped when I muttered those words. She snapped at me a lot—and that's when she chose to notice me at all. I didn't know which was worse.

'Don't be so naïve,' she'd told me. 'Of course, we have guns here! What about farmers, the armed forces, and the IRA? Plus, all the antique ones from years ago.'

I didn't know anyone with a gun (not that I knew many people), and I certainly wouldn't have put farmers in the same category as the IRA, I knew that much.

I got up from the bench, smoothed down my clothes, and paused for a green Vauxhall Viva to pass before crossing the road to catch up with The Texan. My heartbeat thudded in my ears as I wondered if the unsuspecting man could be 'The One'; the person to show me the way.

There had been many potential Ones, though they had all fallen at the last hurdle, plunging me backwards to start my quest again. I tuned out the thumping of excitement in my ears and focused on the task ahead.

I didn't get too close to my possible saviour, but I was near enough to smell the Imperial Leather soap he used, and I knew his clothes were freshly laundered, as the scent gently lingered behind him. Luckily for me, I was also wearing jeans, so I tucked my hands in my pockets and leaned to the left to mimic the innocent stranger who had the potential to turn my life around.

I followed at a steady pace, and if The Texan stopped, so did I. If he bent down to pick up someone's dropped coin, I copied the action, all the while keeping a carefully trained eye on as many reflective surfaces as I could to ensure I could duplicate every move, action, and facial expression.

The shadowing was going well. He had no clue I was following him. He didn't even spot my reflection when he peered into the Aquarius record shop window to examine the new Queen record. I wondered what crossed his mind as he stared at the cover for a moment longer than necessary; perhaps he wanted to buy it, but didn't have enough money.

We were nearly into the housing estate when I was distracted by another man. He didn't look dissimilar from The Texan, except this man wore a donkey jacket with NCB (National Coal Board) embossed on the back, indicating he worked down the local coal mine. Though I had to wonder what he was doing in town; he was far away from the picket line at Hatfield Colliery.

The man walked with purpose in his stride, and I nicknamed him "The Coalman" as I followed. An obvious name, I know. I couldn't smell much from him other than muck and coal. He didn't smell clean like The Texan; it was like his whole body had been engrained with the smell of his job.

Everybody around here supported the miners. When the strikes started, I'd asked my grandad what a picket line meant after seeing it on the news. He explained that they were striking to prevent pit closures.

'Being a miner is a brotherhood,' he informed me. 'They follow the "one out, all out" rule. They gather in front of the gates to the mine, and if anyone passes, they're called *scabs* or *blacklegs*.'

Grandad could provide no explanation for the first name. I imagined the second one was because they still went to work and therefore got dirty from the coal.

I pursued The Coalman all the way to the jobcentre, where he hovered outside and paced the pavement. He looked at a couple of men stood smoking outside before changing his mind and heading back towards the housing estate with his head bent low and the collar on his jacket pulled up high, as though to cover the shame of even contemplating seeking a new job. I knew what he'd considered doing; I didn't need to guess, and I barely knew a thing, as my mum liked to remind me—unless it was about watches. I knew everything about watches.

Grandad once said it can't be nice to struggle to feed your family, as the strikes showed no sign of letting up. Though if anyone should come knocking, he would make sure they had a hot meal and a good, strong mug of tea.

I turned into the estate for my second visit of the day when a police siren forced me to clasp my hands over my ears as the piercing noise shot around my brain like a pinball. I stopped and released my ears, swiftly glancing at the man I'd been following. He peered over his shoulder as the police officer got out of his car and approached the kerb.

The Coalman stared at the police officer, spat on the floor, then carried on. The police and the coalmen hadn't been the best of friends lately; you only had to pick up a paper to read of the clashes between them.

My stomach felt as though it had sunk to my knees, however, and that's where I focused my eyes as the police officer stood in front of me. My body tensed. I knew I was in for a terrible talking to. I'd always tried my best to be discreet and avoid the wrath of PC Williams, but not today, it seems.

'What are you doing, John? How many times am I going to have to drive you home and fill your grandad's heart full of grief?' asked the constable. He tapped his foot as he waited for my reply. I didn't always answer straight away; I needed time to form the answers in my head, or they sometimes came out jumbled—especially if I was nervous or anxious.

'John-Michael it is,' I mumbled. *Crap!* I nearly had it right.

I hated it when others shortened my name. The only people I allowed that honour were my sister Tina, Grandad, our gardener Fred, and Mum (though she rarely did). They didn't shorten it to John, though. Instead, they called me JC.

'What did you say, boy?'

'Officer... Nothing... I wasn't doing anything,' I said. My eyes drifted to my shoes, then to PC Williams's; his shoes hadn't been polished this morning. I could see spots of mud begging to be rubbed off.

I lifted my head a little and inspected the officer's uniform from the neck down for a reflective surface to look into, then sighed with disappointment. I was usually always deflated when I encountered PC Williams. He didn't take care of his uniform like I thought he should. If I were a policeman, I'd have my uniform looking pristine. PC Williams could do with a few cleaning tips, as his buttons weren't shiny. To me, they looked smeary, like they'd been rubbed with margarine or lard.

'Don't be so cheeky, lad. If I didn't know your grandfather so well, you'd be getting a clip around your ear and a size eleven up your arse. I'll ask again, John. Were you following that man over there?' He pointed to The Coalman, who was now disappearing around a corner blissfully unaware of what had been taking place and probably thankful PC Williams had stopped to talk to me instead of him.

I nodded my head.

'I was out working the late shift last night; I really don't need this today,' PC Williams sighed. I guessed he'd been patrolling at the mine.

I paused to choose my words again.

'I'm not hurting anyone, and it isn't a crime,' I said, rubbing the back of my neck. I didn't like where this conversation was heading. I didn't like confrontation. The only things that eased my mind in these situations were reflections, cleaning, or repairing watches. I carried a small cigarette case with a mirror in it in the front left pocket of my Harrington jacket. My grandad had given it to me for these such instances, but I thought better of retrieving it on this occasion. Instead, I twiddled my fingers and hands as though I was washing them, but without soap and water.

I could sense PC Williams considering what I'd said, and I could hear his rough hands stroking the stubble on his chin. He couldn't arrest me, that I was sure of. I hadn't committed a crime; there was no law against walking down the street. But I knew what else he would be thinking—John-Michael is just plain strange.

PC Williams sighed again. 'Why aren't you at work today?' he asked.

'Mr Phillips said he had an important meeting, and I wasn't needed until this afternoon.'

'A meeting with who?' he asked, his surprise evident in the rise of his voice.

'I don't know, officer,' I said, shuffling my feet. I knew it was odd for Claude's Antiques to be closed, but Mr Phillips said he would throw an extra fiver in my wage packet this week for the inconvenience. Though it was hardly an inconvenience to me; it meant I got extra time doing my hobbies. 'He hasn't shared any details of the business with me yet. I just repair the watches and clocks and go home. I'm supposed to learn soon, though.'

'Has he been acting strange lately?' PC Williams asked.

I bit my lip at that word. It was funny he was asking me if my boss had been acting strange when everyone thought I was the strange one in town.

I couldn't exactly be sure of what he meant by *strange*, either; what's strange to one person might be totally normal to another.

'Well, define strange?' I said.

'Closing early, meetings, odd phone calls, secrecy…' the constable rattled off.

I hummed and shrugged. 'I'm not sure.'

Though, I was sure. I just wasn't certain if it was my place to tell PC Williams. What if he told Mr Phillips, and I was sacked due to my lack of discretion? Plus, Mum always said not to tell tales. No, I couldn't tell him.

Really, Mr Phillips *had* been different these past few weeks, ever since his last house clearance. I'd heard raised voices in the shop and on the phone, but whenever I'd popped my head out to investigate, the person had either left or Mr Phillips hung up the phone. He'd also been in and out of his office, checking his safe more regularly, and a couple of times I found him asleep at his desk and he'd forgotten to lock up.

I heard PC Williams scratch his chin again. 'Alright. Get in the car, and I'll take you home.'

I exhaled loudly, thankful the interrogation was over, and climbed into the back of the car. I was pleased in one way; at least now I could look at the officer through the rear-view mirror. The constable got in and immediately eyed me through the mirror as I knew he would.

'What we going to do about you,' PC Williams said.

It didn't sound like a question, but I couldn't be sure.

I chose not to reply and looked at the officer's eyes in the mirror; they were a cloudy-blue colour with flecks of green and rimmed red due to lack of sleep. I recognised the familiar effect from my own eyes; I found it hard to sleep at times because my brain often didn't shut down at night.

I kept my eyes steadfast on the rear-view mirror, but shifted a little as the air remained silent for too long. 'You know… I'm not hurting anyone,' I said, repeating my earlier statement. 'I'm only minding my own business.'

'Doesn't look that way to me. If you end up following any of them ruffians and they spot you, you'll be in for a kicking.'

Visions of thugs and gangsters coming at me with their fists and legs flailing about flew through my mind. I would be careful and make sure his warning never happened.

'They won't spot me. I always have my head down and keep to myself,' I said. The townsfolk had spotted me following others on the odd occasion, but I would usually dive into an alleyway or shop doorway if I thought I'd been noticed. But nobody ever said anything to me. In fact, no one really spoke to me at all.

'Oh really?' the constable asked, drumming his hairy fingers on the battered steering wheel. 'Really?' he repeated. 'What about the last time I took you home, aye?'

'Oh...,' I mumbled. 'That was... unfortunate.'

The incident PC Williams was speaking of happened last year in the summer of eighty-three. I'd been following a woman when I accidentally tripped over a loose flagstone and went hurtling through the air towards her. I reached out to grab something to stop myself from hitting the pavement, and I ended up grabbing her skirt and pulling it down. She called me words that I'd only heard on *The Sweeney*, causing a massive scene.

Unluckily for me, PC Williams had been nearby. I'd had a tough time explaining the incident when I got home. Mum was so angry, she clipped me round the ear, and Grandad shook his head and disappeared into his office until he was ready to speak to me about it.

Grandad walked me to and from work for a week after that, and Mum dragged me to the doctors in an attempt to get me 'fixed.' He just said I was a little different and a bit anti-social.

The incident was the sole reason I no longer followed women. And children, you may ask? Well, I never followed them. I might not have known a lot, but even I knew that was a big no-no. Besides, children didn't know who they were yet.

'Why do you do it? Can you at least tell me that much?' PC Williams had asked me this question before, and I always gave the same answer.

'I'm looking for something,' I whispered.

'Looking for what?' He glanced over his shoulder to look at me.

'I'm not sure… I'll know when I've found it…' I trailed off.

'I think you just need to find some friends.'

People often asked me why I was the way I was, but I was never able to give them a reason. It was like a compulsion, and I couldn't tell them what it was I was searching for exactly in The One, either. All I knew was I had something missing, and somebody out there had what I needed to make me whole again.

When I found what it was, I'd shout the answer to the whole world. Then maybe Mum and Grandad would stop fretting about me for a while.

The officer exhaled loudly. 'You are one odd lad,' he tried to mutter under his breath. I'd heard that term, *odd*, loads of times; it didn't hurt so much anymore, but there were still some words that could sting my eyes.

'You want to be giving up this following malarkey. Get yourself some friends, a girlfriend, a full-time job, and stop wasting my time and yours.'

'I'm not wasting my time,' I said, rolling my eyes and turning my gaze to the window.

'What's she doing on her own?'

The car slowed, and I looked to the opposite window to see an approaching WPC. It was indeed peculiar to see a female officer out on her own. This WPC was slim but had a swagger in her stride, as though she would start running at any minute. She had a round, smiling face, and you could just see her dark hair peeking out from under her hat. I'd seen her before, and I liked her. Well, her clothes, anyway. Her uniform was pristine.

PC Williams pulled over and wound down the passenger-side window. 'What's all this, lacy legs? Where's Thomas at?'

'He's getting some fags. He said he'll catch up in a minute, sir.'

Everyone called PC Williams *sir*. He wasn't a senior officer, so his colleagues didn't need to, but he was the longest serving and most experienced officer in the station—that's what Grandad told me, anyway. He had a lot of respect in the community, and if he told you to do something, you did it.

He scoffed. 'He's most likely gone to see his fancy piece round the corner. He shouldn't be letting you walk around on your own.'

'I know. I'm sorry, sir,' she said, though she didn't sound particularly sorry to me.

I looked back to the rear-view mirror to watch their exchange.

'Hey'—PC Williams waved his hand—'no need to apologise to me. It's you that'll be sorry if any of them low lives see you out and about on your own.'

'Yes, sir.'

'Get in. I'll take you back to the station once I've dropped off young John here.'

It's John-Michael! My brain shouted. How many times did I have to tell him?

PC Williams moved his helmet from the passenger seat and chucked it over his shoulder to make room for her. I tutted under my breath as it landed next to me. It could have easily hit me.

'Hey, John-Michael,' the WPC said.

'Hello,' I mumbled, my eyes now firmly focused on my hands folded in my lap.

I knew the WPC from around town. She was only a few years older than my twenty-one years. I didn't speak to girls often; I was too self-conscious. But they probably wouldn't go out with me, anyway.

'What's he done?' she asked PC Williams.

'He's been following someone again. I'm going to have a quick word with his grandfather,' he replied.

I switched off from their conversation then. I was used to being talked about, even if I was in the same room. Mum was the worst culprit for it. I used my brain as a radio or record player when I needed to escape. I would swap the channels around in my head when I was uncomfortable. I placed an album on the imaginary record player in my mind and lost myself in the sounds of The Beat's *I Just Can't Stop It*.

I mumbled along to *Mirror in the Bathroom*. It was my favourite song on the album, not only because they sang about mirrors and reflections but because the song resonated with me somehow, somewhere deep inside me.

The WPC shifted in the passenger seat and turned to look at me. I looked out the window again. 'What's with the mumbling about a bathroom, John-Michael? Do you need the toilet, or something?'

'No,' I muttered.

Why would I tell them I needed the toilet?

'You want to get yourself a girlfriend,' she sniggered. 'Instead of loitering about. Have you ever spoken to a girl 'cept for me?'

I ignored her and carried on listening to my record.

'Give over now. Leave him alone,' said PC Williams.

'Alright, sorry, sir,' said WPC Thompson, still giggling to herself.

I didn't know why she was laughing. I didn't think she had a boyfriend; I hadn't seen her name written on any of the benches around town.

I balanced my elbow on the car door and rested my chin on my hand to gaze out the window. But I turned off my internal jukebox as a strange man caught my eye. A shiver ran right through me at the sight of him. He wasn't walking; he was slinking, the same way a cat stalks a bird. He was in our town hunting his prey, the same way I was searching for the person who would unlock the secret to making me whole.

He was the same height and build as me, with chestnut hair, and he was tanned, as though he'd been on holiday to Spain for a month. He wore a shiny dark-blue suit that seemed to change colour when the light hit it—almost like a shark, I thought. It had a small collar and three buttons going down—the bottom one was left undone. His trousers were narrowly fitted, and a silky red tie protruded at his neck. The outfit was completed by a three-pointed hanky sticking out of his top pocket. He looked like a sixties Italian film star, earning him the perfect nickname: "The Suit."

He didn't belong here.

Though no one else saw him—not even PC Williams, who was usually so observant. I moved to look out the rear window, but he'd disappeared. If I'd been on foot, I would have followed him. He didn't belong here, but I couldn't put my finger on why. It wasn't just that his clothes were out of place here; there was something else...

I folded my arms in a huff and waited to arrive home.

CHAPTER TWO

FOR THE REST OF the journey, I focused on my companions' conversation and more importantly, their thoughts. I liked to envisage what people pondered in their brains as the cogs turned, just like watches. If what I imagined up was interesting enough, it would get an entry in my journal.

I bet PC Williams was considering why Mr Phillips had shut the shop this morning, and as though he'd read my mind, too, PC Williams spoke up.

'Say, have you been down the high street today?' he asked WPC Thompson.

'No, sir. Why do you ask?'

He hummed. 'Claude closed the antique shop this morning. He never shuts...' He trailed off.

She shrugged. 'Maybe he had a meeting.'

'Not likely,' he said, shaking his head.

I had to agree. Everyone knew Mr Phillips never closed. Even if he was ill, he somehow summoned the strength to roll out of bed, trundle downstairs, and lift the shutters.

The fact PC Williams was thinking about Mr Phillips made me think about him too. Perhaps I needed to pay more attention to how he was acting. He might be in trouble and need my help.

He'd never kept secrets from me before, but then I hadn't outright questioned him about it.

I'd ask him about his meeting as soon as I got to work. Maybe if I got my head out of the watches for a time, I could figure out what was going on.

I switched my attention to WPC Thompson. I supposed she was thinking about the PC who had left her to walk the street alone. It was easy to guess where he was; off riding the town-bike. I'd heard Mum and several of her friends talking about the town-bike. The gossip was that PC Thomas Brown loved the town-bike, though I'd never seen it for myself.

I often wondered what model the famous town-bike was. I liked to imagine it as a BMX, but I couldn't picture the policeman on a BMX, so I narrowed my options down to a racer; a red one.

The car turned onto Rosemary Drive and pulled up at the end of our long driveway. We lived on the outskirts of town between Thorne and Moorends on the edge of the peat moors. There were only a few other houses here. Grandad said when the house was first built, the street didn't have a name, as it was mainly disused farmland.

'Here we are, lad, let's go have a word with your grandfather, shall we?'

'Yes, sir.' I glanced towards the house, checking for any movement. I wasn't looking forward to this one bit and secretly hoped no one was home. I straightened the collar on my jacket to stall for time as PC Williams opened the car door, then walked around to the other side.

'Won't be long, love, ten minutes tops,' he said to WPC Thompson as he retrieved his helmet.

'Alright, sir.'

Off we sauntered down the drive, and I kept a step behind him as we made our way. We didn't speak as we walked; all that could be heard were the birds singing in the trees and the sound of the gravel crunching underneath our feet. I kept my head down now we were out of the car and I no longer had the rear-view mirror to look into.

Our house had been built over a hundred and fifty years ago and had been in the family ever since. At the roadside stood a garage and a showroom, though it had closed five years earlier. The house itself was set back from the road in the middle of a modest three-acre plot of land. A small cottage sat at the back for the gamekeeper. Our gardener lived in it now—for free, as Mum pointed out regularly. He took care of the gardens and was employed by others around town to do theirs. Fred was a close family friend. Even though he was a lot older than me, I spent a lot of time in his company. He'd been one of my dad's best mates.

Grandad must have heard us crunching along the loose gravel, as he emerged from the garage. I looked up slightly and watched as he wiped his greasy hands on his overalls; he seemed to be shaking his head as he approached us.

'Hey, Steve,' the officer said cheerfully as I hovered behind him.

'Hello, my dear friend,' Grandad said, extending an arm to shake his hand. Then he turned to me. 'Wait for me in the kitchen,' he said.

'Yes, Grandad,' I replied and walked slowly towards the house.

'I'm sorry you've had to bring him home again. What's he done now?'

I lingered by the door at an angle to avoid their faces and to listen to what the constable had to say about me.

'Hey, no apology necessary. I'm just looking out for the lad, is all. I know you'd do the same for my boys.'

Grandad nodded his agreement.

'I caught him following some man down the street,' the constable added.

'I see. I'll have another word with him.'

'Aye, I know you will, pal. So, how's the family keeping?' PC Williams asked.

'You know how it is. Money's tight, and I miss the family and everything we had going for us. Ten years later, and I still expect Alex and Barb to come walking through the door any minute. And our John-Michael is the spit of him,' he said, wiping at his mouth.

I knew times were tough. Grandad Stephen Chester couldn't run the garage in his advancing years. His son and my father, Alex Chester, died twelve years ago when I was nine. He was only thirty-six, and I still missed him. Grandad had wanted me to take over the garage when I was old enough, but I wasn't interested in car mechanics. The only mechanics I was interested in were that of watches. Grandad said it was his fault I had no interest in cars, because he had spent hours teaching me how to repair watches. Though he was proud I'd become the best horologist he knew, besides him.

'I can see that, pal. No mistaking who his dad was except for them baby blues. Pulls at your heartstrings, doesn't it?'

Grandad sighed loudly and nodded.

'And Anna? How's she doing? Any better?'

'Hardly, she's going to flip when she hears about this. She's awful to him. Anyone can see he's not quite right. And I can't forgive her for all things she's said to him over the years. She's partially to blame for the way he turned out, in my opinion. I wish the doctors had got to the bottom of it all those years ago.'

PC Williams patted him on the shoulder, and I slumped back against the wall. I knew exactly what he was referring to. I remember Mum telling me my eyes were the cause of all my problems. She said they unnerved people, and they wouldn't look at me, and in time, I stopped looking at them too. I could gaze at the rest of their bodies and quickly glance at their faces if they weren't looking in my direction, but that was about it. I wish I knew what was wrong with me. Maybe I could learn how to fix it, and I'd be accepted by everyone, but especially by Mum.

'Do you want to come in for a quick cuppa?' Grandad asked him. 'Or something stronger?'

'Sure. Go on, then, a wee drop won't hurt.'

'Aye, good man.'

I ran through the side door to the kitchen, quickly filled the kettle, and placed it on the stove. Grandad and PC Williams entered a couple of moments later. I spied them from the many mirrors and reflective surfaces I'd positioned around the house. The constable's eyes grew wide. No matter how many times he'd been in our house, his reaction was still the same.

On my last count, we had a hundred and sixty-seven mirrors in our house—twelve of those were in the kitchen. Our house was quite big, and despite its size, it was spotless. Every pot, pan, mirror, and surface in the kitchen had been scrubbed by me until it sparkled, as had everything reflective in all the other rooms.

I gazed at the picture of my dad pinned above the stove as I waited for the kettle to whistle. Mum liked it there to look at while she cooked. Grandad was right; I looked exactly like him. I was tall and slim like he had been, though I didn't know what *spitting* had to do with the way I looked (I didn't spit; it was a disgusting habit). But it was true, I did resemble him even more so now I was older—apart from my eyes. No one had eyes like mine. Dad had hazel eyes and chestnut hair like Grandad, though Grandad's hair had been feathered with grey—almost white—for some time now. Mum had bottle-green eyes, as did my sister Tina, and they both had blonde hair that curled at the ends. Tina and I had both inherited olive skin from Grandad's Italian heritage, too, which only made my eyes stand out even more.

PC Williams seated himself at the small wooden table while grandad poured two thumb-sized measures of whiskey into small tumblers. The constable swiftly scanned the room as he waited, catching a glimpse of himself in a mirror, then turned away.

What had he seen that he didn't like? Perhaps it was the advancing years creeping up on him. Mum said the mirrors reminded her she was losing her youth. I wondered if that was her reason behind breaking one now and again.

'Here you go, pal.' Grandad placed a glass down in front of the officer.

'Cheers.'

They raised their glasses and took big gulps, then savoured the burn as the golden liquid glided down their throats and into their stomachs. Grandad had let me try a glass when I turned eighteen. I didn't enjoy it, therefore I rarely drank, nor did I frequent the many pubs like most lads my age. I had no one my age to go with, anyway, even if I wanted to.

I had a couple of mates. Well… *mates* was stretching it a bit; they were acquaintances, really. We had bonded somehow over the unique social awkwardness we shared. Carl had teenage acne that refused to disappear. I'd expressed he should wash his face every morning and evening with soap, but I didn't know if he followed my advice. Then there was Paul. He had a terrible stammer and so hardly spoke.

I brought over my cup of steaming hot tea and sat with them to await the lecture I was about to receive. I shuffled into position so I could see the reflections of the men sat in front of me.

Grandad took another sip of his whiskey, then sucked his cheeks in before he spoke, no doubt wondering what to say this time to get me to change my ways.

'John-Michael, you know why PC Williams brought you home today, don't you?'

I nodded, though the action didn't mean I agreed. In my opinion, I hadn't done a thing wrong. Not one foot out of line. It wasn't as though I was a criminal.

'You know it's not that we want to stop you from doing what you enjoy... Perhaps, if you told us why you do it or what you're looking for, we could help?' he said, looking to his friend for assistance.

I remained still and silent.

I couldn't tell them what I was looking for exactly; it was hard for me to put into words. I was looking for something that was missing within me, and I hoped I could spot it within someone else.

'We're just looking out for you, John, is all,' the constable said. 'We don't want you getting into trouble—and I don't just mean with the police. There're a lot of stran... funny buggers about.'

I blinked back at them from the mirror. I'd had enough of their threats and reasoning. I would think about what they had said, but that would be it. I knew I would probably have another talking to once Mum found out, anyway, and I wasn't looking forward to the fallout from that.

'Is it the clothes you're attracted to when you're following them?' Grandad asked.

I shrugged. 'No, I've got my own clothes.'

'Well, at least he's not cross-dressing like Les Dawson,' PC Williams said, then they both laughed. I didn't know if they were laughing at me or at what he'd said.

'Can you imagine our John-Michael's hair in curlers with a hairnet on?' said Grandad.

They laughed some more, and I interrupted, eager to get on with my day.

'I'll take into consideration what you've both said, thank you. If you don't mind, I'm going to get ready for work,' I said to the mirror, then walked away, my mug of tea left steaming on the table.

'We shouldn't be laughing, really,' I heard PC Williams say.

I hovered in the passageway and stood where I could see them, but they couldn't see me. I knew every angle of every mirror and reflective surface in the house.

The duo both sighed and finished their drinks simultaneously.

'I really don't know what else I can do,' Grandad said, shaking his head.

'I dunno, pal. All we can do is look out for them and do our best. I best be off now; got a young WPC waiting in the car,' PC Williams said, getting up. 'I'll see myself out. Thanks for the tipple.'

'Anytime, mate…' Grandad trailed off, then slammed his fist down on the table when his friend was out of earshot.

CHAPTER THREE

I TURNED THE CORNER onto the street where I worked in time to see The Suit standing outside the hardware shop almost opposite Claude's Antiques. He stood tall with his chin tilted up as he straightened his tie and ran a hand through his hair. To any onlooker, he appeared to be examining the pans and brushes on display, but I knew different. He was keeping an eye on the antique shop behind him.

The hairs on the back of my neck stood on end. I didn't know what it was about this man, but his existence in our town filled me with dread. Was he the gentleman Claude was having a meeting with? He seemed too fancy for our little town; his suit looked more expensive than everything in both shops combined.

A car horn pipped down the street, and he looked left and right in apparent shock. I made to cross the road but couldn't find a big enough gap in the traffic. A pedestrian knocked me with their elbow and yelled, "Watch where you're going, son!" causing people to stare, and I had to force myself to carry on to avoid being in people's ways.

I paused merely feet away from The Suit. His position had changed; his head was bent to the left, and he was staring intently at me through the window's reflection. I bowed my head and attempted to cross again.

Before stepping into the road, something made me take a final glance at The Suit's mirror image. His upper lip curled into a malicious grin, forcing another shiver down my spine, then he swivelled round and marched down the street in the opposite direction.

If it wouldn't have made me late, I'd have followed him. His presence unnerved me. I'd seen him twice now and been unable to follow him on both occasions. I was desperate to find out who he was. However, despite my curiosity, I hoped he wouldn't be around for long.

I continued to the shop and opened the door. The ever-present aroma hit me before the bell rang. I loved the smell in Claude's Antiques. Mr Phillips smoked a pipe, and the scent of it mixed in with the polish I used to clean everything.

As the bell above the door chimed, Mr Phillips jumped from his ledger, then focused his eyes back on the numbers on the page when he saw it was me. I paused at the threshold in horror. The counter was in a state of disarray; he had two phone books open, plus the yellow pages. His Rolodex cardholder was out (which held the details of customers and other antique dealers), and at least twenty of the cards were scattered across the worktop. I'd never seen things so disorganised.

I wondered why he had jumped too. I'd never seen him do that before. Was he frightened of something? I didn't think anything could scare Mr Phillips.

'Afternoon, John-Michael,' he said, not looking up.

'Hello, Mr Phillips,' I said. 'Would you… like any help looking for something?'

'No, thank you. I think I've got it covered,' he said.

I scratched my head as I searched for something else to say. 'Can I help you tidy up, then?'

'No, I'm good.'

'Oh okay. Umm… so, the meeting… How did it go?'

He set down his pencil but still didn't raise his head. He exhaled loudly. 'You don't need to worry about that, laddie. You just keep repairing them watches. I'll take care of everything else.'

'Yes, sir.'

I shook my head as I approached my workbench. I had left it clean and tidy when I finished on Saturday, and now a small box of trinkets sat on it with three watches and a mantel clock, waiting to be repaired.

I lifted the box and placed it with some others tucked away in the corner, then I carefully placed the watches on a small cushion I kept under the bench so I could set up my working area.

I grabbed a duster and gave my mirrors a wipe. I worked in the back of the shop, and Claude had let me position mirrors and reflective surfaces where I saw fit and to make my hours there comfortable. People came from miles around to have their watches repaired by me. I'd also started repairing mantel clocks and would soon progress to bigger ones. Word had spread quickly about my skills; I had fast become the most sought-after horologist around. The knowledge made me feel really special, like I was needed and wanted in some way. I wasn't needed or accepted anywhere else.

First, I took out a white cloth from my top drawer and placed it on the bench, smoothing out the creases as I did so. Next, I opened the second drawer and removed all my tools and carefully set them out in the order I would be using them. Lastly, I retrieved my loupes from the bottom drawer; these were the magnifying devices I used. Two were given to me by my grandfather, and the other, Claude had given me. I had the white cloth so I could see all the pieces clearly and the parts were easier to find should I drop them with the delicate brass tweezers.

Before I started, I made us both a strong and sweet cup of tea. Claude had four sugars in his, and I had two. There was a mini kitchen in the back next to the storage room with a sink and a hotplate stove. Before the kitchen was the door that led upstairs. Mr Phillips lived alone in the small flat above the shop. His wife Mary had died three years earlier. Mr and Mrs Phillips hadn't had any children of their own. However, they did have nieces and nephews, though they lived in Australia. He'd never met them in person, but he did get a photo of them every year, which he took pride in showing me.

I made the teas and set Mr Phillips's mug at the side of his ledger. He didn't acknowledge my presence; he was engrossed in searching through his Rolodex.

'Here's your tea, Mr Phillips,' I said.

He flinched when he heard my voice, then shook his head. 'Oh, thanks, John-Michael,' he said, abandoning his search to shuffle some papers before putting them under the counter so I couldn't see them.

'Mr Phillips, I was thinking…'

'Hmm, what about?' he said, moving to shut his ledger.

'Well, we've known each other for a long time. How about you call me JC now, if you'd like?'

'I'd like that,' he said. I looked towards the mirror nearest to him and saw he was smiling at me.

'Great.' I turned to leave but stopped. His jumpiness and the mess on the counter had me curious.

'Did you have a good meeting, then, Mr Phillips? It must have been pretty important to shut all morning.' I shuffled my feet on the wooden floor as I spoke. I wasn't used to questioning him, so I had to proceed with caution.

'Well, see'n as though you've asked… again. A potential buyer wanted to see me about some rare antiquities I've got my hands on. But he's not quite right for them. Plus, I've got a collector in mind.'

'How rare? Is it a watch?' I tilted my head and tapped my lip with my index finger.

'Never you mind, that's for me to worry about. Get yourself started on them watches,' he said, waving me off.

'But, Mr Phillips, I thought we didn't have secrets from each other, and you said the other week I needed to start learning more about the business side,' I said.

'That's right, we don't, lad. But it won't be around long enough for you to see or concern yourself with. Okay?'

'Okay…'

I stomped back to my work area and roughly pulled out my chair, banging it on the floor. It frustrated me that no one ever discussed important topics with me, as though they thought me too young to hear what they had to say. How was I meant to learn the business if Claude didn't share important details with me? And I hated that I was never allowed to participate in adult conversations, like any input from me would be irrelevant. After all, I was an adult now—old enough to drink, vote, work, and have a girlfriend. Just because I acted differently to everyone else didn't mean I didn't understand things. I wasn't stupid.

And no, perhaps I wasn't *normal* in their eyes, but what was normal, anyway? Who decided that?

I knew what was going on at home. Grandad was worried about money and how he would continue to keep the roof over our heads without having to sell more of his beloved car collection. I had offered to pay lodge out of my wages, but he refused, said he wouldn't hear of it. I told him he had heard me, because I'd just told him, but he waved me away.

Sometimes I wish I could have gone into car mechanics like the rest of the men in my family, and maybe Grandad wouldn't have had to sell his cherished cars. Perhaps I could do both? I would have to think about it. I knew my way around a car engine. Of course, I did. So did my sister. But I'd turned away from cars and bikes when Grandad first sat me down and showed me the insides of a watch. I couldn't believe how many components and mechanisms made up such a small object. It looked so complex; I had to know how it all fit together.

And now something was going on in Claude's Antiques.

It was about time I became more involved in the adult world. Especially if it were to affect the shop. I worked here, too, and I'd be lost without my job here. It gave me purpose, a routine. And most of all, it kept me out of Mum's way.

I started on the first watch while I thought of the secret antique and the mystery man who loitered outside. I wondered if they were connected.

CHAPTER FOUR

I FINISHED WORK AT five and went to find Mr Phillips. I spotted him in his office bent in front of his large safe. Inside was a large red case I'd never seen before, and I'd seen most of the inventory that had come through the shop in the last eight years. I'd had a Saturday job here until I finished my exams. Then he'd upped my hours.

'Goodnight, Mr Phillips.'

He jumped and slammed the safe shut, grunting something at me.

'See you Thursday. Don't forget to lock up,' I said with a frown before leaving. What was in that safe he didn't want me to see?

I decided to take a shortcut home through the medieval orchard between the shops. The orchard belonged to the town's castle centuries ago. It was gone now; only the odd bit of stone and timber remained, but the orchard and moat endured.

The trees had started to blossom, and I enjoyed the sweet smell as I walked through them. It wouldn't be long before people would come to pick the fruit for their pies and jams. Nana B used to bake using the apples here. She died, too, just before Dad died. People didn't stay around long enough for my liking. Did people really not want to look at me like Mum said? Is that why they died? To get away from me? I shook the thought away. It didn't feel nice in my stomach to think that way, so I focused on my surroundings instead.

I liked walking through here; when there was no one else around, I could keep my head up and see the sun beaming through the old branches. The trees were ancient—probably as old as the castle would have been if it were still standing. The branches were old and gnarly, twisting around like vines. When I was younger, I would imagine the branches sweeping me up and lifting me high above the town to see what no one else had the pleasure of witnessing.

As I exited the orchard, I dropped into the moat, which had been cleared of muck and water the year before. It was a common hangout for kids from the nearby grammar school to hide and smoke in at lunchtime. I'd seen them loitering a couple of times. I'd never tried a cigarette or even kicked a football around.

I was expelled when I was ten, not long after my father's death. It wasn't because of that, nor was it because I'd been naughty or disruptive, in my opinion. The reason the school had given was due to an unfortunate incident with a boy in my class named Joe; the incident resulted in him having a broken nose. Though I hadn't laid one finger on him.

I'd bent down to pick up a book, and as I rose back up, I saw Joe's reflection in the glass of the door, poised like a tiger ready to pounce. As Joe moved, I ducked and rolled out of the way, resulting in Joe colliding face-first with the door.

It wasn't my fault. When I look back on it now, I think the school just wanted to be rid of me. They said they didn't know how to teach someone like me. I had no idea what that had meant at the time. In fact, I still don't. I could be taught, I just didn't want to look at people. What was unteachable about that?

As I walked, I didn't bother looking for someone to follow as I normally would have done. All I could think about was

Claude's Antiques and what I should do next to get to the bottom of the mystery. Maybe if I could unravel it, I'd be accepted into the adult world and people would treat me as such, instead of a child. Would solving it take me one step closer to who I should be?

I arrived at the house to the sound of my mum listening to the *Eurythmics* in the front room. That room was hers; it didn't have as many mirrors as other rooms. She said she wanted a bit of normalcy in at least one part of the house besides her bedroom. The front room had a peach, three-piece suite, a wall unit with a drink's cabinet inside (though it never had any bottles in it), and a couple of framed pictures of Mum and Dad on their wedding day.

I watched her thin frame from the reflection in a mirror. She slowly swayed and mumbled along to the music, a glass of wine clutched in one hand and a cigarette in the other. I missed seeing her dance with dad. He would pick her up and twirl her around as they listened to the record player, and she'd be laughing and yelling at the same time, asking him to put her down. Then he would spin her before dipping her backwards to give her a kiss.

That's when everything was good, when mum used to smile, though not at me. She was young and beautiful back then. She didn't smile now; she wore a permanent frown, and she'd stopped wearing makeup. I left her to it and headed up to my room to write in my journal.

I'd bought the journal to keep a record of all the people I'd followed over the years. It was thick and heavy, and I'd wrapped twenty elastic bands tightly around it. The journal lived concealed in my wardrobe; there was a drawer at the bottom which I removed and hid items underneath.

I started with The Texan—how he'd walked, what he'd looked at—then moved on to The Coalman. Then I wrote everything I could remember about The Suit and where I'd seen him. He was the most important entry in my journal to date. I even underlined his name three times to indicate his importance.

Downstairs, the phone rang, and I closed my journal and returned it to its hiding place. Then I lay on my bed and stared up at the ceiling where I'd placed my favourite Bruce Lee poster from *Enter the Dragon*. Our gardener Fred had told me all about Bruce Lee, and we'd watched his films together on his little black-and-white television. Sometimes I spoke to Bruce, asked him what he would do in my shoes, though he never answered me. I think I'd be quite taken aback if he ever did.

I'd been on my bed for all of a minute when I heard Mum shouting for me to come down. I hadn't even realised she had acknowledged my presence when I arrived home from work.

As I walked into the lounge, I knew I was about to get another talk about this morning's police car ride. She only ever called me down to speak to her when I'd done something wrong.

'Care to explain why you were seen getting a ride home with the police this morning, John-Michael?' she asked with a hand on her hip which jutted out through her skirt. She'd grown thinner since Dad died.

'I wasn't doing anything wrong, Mum. PC Williams gave me a lift home,' I told her reflection as I twiddled my hands behind my back.

'The police don't just give free rides,' she said, walking over to the record player to lift up the arm. 'They're not a taxi service, John-Michael. Do you know how embarrassing it is to hear all about it from Mrs Nosey-Nelly?'

I rubbed at my head as I searched through my memory, trying to identify who this woman was. I came up blank.

'Who's Mrs Nosey-Nelly? Do I know her?'

'It's Mrs Kelly. Don't change the subject.'

'Then why did you call her Mrs Nosey-Nelly?'

Mum sighed loudly, then slumped into her favourite seat, almost spilling her drink as she went down. 'Do I have to explain every tiny detail of everything I say? God, I'm sick of it.'

I opened my mouth to respond, but she interrupted: 'Is there anything in that brain of yours? Do you have the slightest comprehension of how your actions affect me?'

Her voice rose and rose in pitch until it would only be audible to the dogs roaming the streets. Heat rose to my face, just as it seemed to in hers. I backed up to the door, then turned and ran.

Her voice came down a notch as she shouted, 'That's it! Go running off to your grandad, like a baby!'

Tears pooled in my eyes, blurring my vision as I found my way through the house. You would think I'd have got used to it by now—the jabs and snide comments. They were always worse when she'd been drinking.

I burst into Grandad's office without knocking.

'She's at it again!' I yelled at my grandad's reflection in the mirror to my right.

Grandad sighed, set down the newspaper he'd been reading, and looked back at me in the mirror.

'It's not *she*—that's the cat's mother. And what over this time?' he asked.

I stepped inside, letting the door swing closed behind me. 'Sorry, Grandad, and sorry for not knocking too.'

'That's alright, John-Michael. Just don't forget next time. Tell me what's wrong,' he said, folding his arms on the desk in front of him.

'Mum was listening to her records, then she got a call from Mrs Kelly—do you know Mum calls her Mrs Nosey-Nelly?' I asked him, switching my attention to the mirror on my left.

'Focus on what you wanted to tell me, John-Michael.'

'Oh right, yes. She shouted me down and asked me why I'd got a lift home in the police car this morning. I told her I hadn't done anything wrong, which is the truth—'

The sound of breaking glass echoed down the hall, making me flinch. I couldn't bear the noise of shattering glass. 'Not one of my mirrors again…' I groaned, wiping at my head as my brow furrowed.

'It can be replaced, you know this. Now, you stay here until I come back,' Grandad said, slowly rising from his brown leather chair. His bones clicked and popped as he stood. I'd told him numerous times he should see a doctor, but he'd told me he had a feeling his joints needed replacing and there was no way he could be off his feet. Plus, he didn't trust doctors, anymore. Not after Dad.

I moved the opposite way round the desk to avoid his path, and as he closed the door behind him, I sank into the newly vacated plush leather seat. He'd got it from Claude's Antiques with a hefty discount.

I loved this room; Grandad had made sure there were enough reflections for me to look into. Any reflective surface would suffice—people's glasses, cutlery, shop windows, puddles—but I favoured mirrors above all.

My family catered to my needs as much as they could, though they didn't understand it. They all told me my strange habit had affected them all in some way, but especially Mum. Everything seemed to affect Mum the worst.

Loud voices drifting through the walls made me sink back into the chair. Raised voices only meant one thing in this house; they were arguing about me. I was one of the two things they argued about most: me and money. They had been this way ever since Dad died; a day I will never forget. A day that changed all our lives forever. Tina said Mum and Grandad fought like cats and dogs. I asked her who was what. She said mum was the cat.

I couldn't bear listening to them fighting all the time—especially when I didn't know what they were saying. Hadn't I just promised myself I would convince them I'm just as much of an adult as they are?

I slammed my hands down on the desk and forced the chair back. I wasn't going to sit here and hide away, anymore. I got up and went down the hall to listen to their shouts; if it was about me, why shouldn't I listen?

'I can't stand him being trapped in a world of mirrors and reflections!' Mum shouted. 'Do you think anything of this is normal?'

It went silent for a moment, then I heard another mirror smash. I bit down on my lip. That was two I would have to buy tomorrow.

'Anna, it's not the boy's fault,' Grandad said. 'He's got problems. You've never even tried to get to know the boy properly. He's a good lad. I swear the only time you were interested was when he passed his exams.'

Grandad was right. When I got kicked out of the local school, the next nearest school wouldn't admit me, and the bus didn't come close enough for the one after that. Home-schooling became my only option.

Grandad found some great tutors for me, and all three of them managed the mirror situation well. Mr Spencer taught me all the science subjects, Mrs Forrester taught me English and Maths, and Mr Woods taught me Geography and History. They only taught me for a couple of hours a day—I found I couldn't concentrate well for much longer than that. They all said I was a good student, and I passed all seven O-level exams with a C grade. It was the only time Mum had ever expressed any sort of pride in me.

'He took my dreams away!' Mum shouted.

I chewed on the inside of my cheek and headed back to the office. I'd heard enough.

The voices coming from the room got louder as I crept back. Mum was madder than ever. In an attempt to forget what was happening a few metres away from me, I put on my internal record player, picked up a duster, and got to work on polishing all the reflective surfaces.

CHAPTER FIVE

GRANDAD CAME BACK HALF an hour later, though the voices had died down sometime before. I could always count on him to calm her down, eventually.

'How's it going in here, son?' he asked.

'Good, Grandad. I've dusted everything. Not a speck of dirt or a smear anywhere,' I said proudly.

'Good lad. Your mam has calmed down now, and she's getting tea on. Why don't you go see if she needs a hand?'

'I need to check the mirrors she smashed first, then I will. I'll come get you when it's ready.'

'Alright, son.' He smiled at me in the mirror, then quickly looked away.

I went to inspect the damage. Mum had smashed one of my favourite Art Deco mirrors. I shook my head, then waved the sadness away. I couldn't let her see she'd upset me twice in the space of an hour.

I noticed a small sliver of glass on the floor. Every time Mum smashed one of the mirrors, she always swept up the pieces and disposed of the remnants, though she never offered to replace them, nor did she ever apologise.

I bent to pick up the shard, and a sharp edge nicked my finger. I quickly sucked the red bead that formed and grabbed a plaster from my wallet. I always kept a supply handy for two reasons: one, I hated the sight of blood (the quicker I could stop the bleeding the better), and two, I'd lost count of the number of times I'd cut myself on broken glass.

I composed myself until I spotted the other mirror she'd smashed. It was the ornate silver mirror Mr Phillips let me have. It had been in his storage area for years and was filthy. I'd taken it home and spent hours on it with a duster and a can of Mr Sheen, working in all the grooves and crevices to remove every speck of dust and grime. When I was done, it had looked beautiful and wouldn't have been out of place in a stately home.

I rubbed at my eyes, scrubbing away the tears threatening to spill over. I knew I shouldn't cry over a mirror; Mum had said often enough. *Boys don't cry.* I never let her see me cry, and I tried my hardest not to let her actions or words get to me.

Sometimes I felt as though I could, *should*, shout and scream back at my mother for acting the way she did, but I forced the screams down that rose from my stomach into my chest and locked them away. Both Tina and Grandad said she didn't mean it, but I wasn't so sure. I didn't see her smashing up any of their stuff on a regular basis.

I took a deep breath and walked into the kitchen. Mum was peeling potatoes with mince sizzling in a pan on the stove. Her wine glass had been topped back up. I disposed of the shard of glass and stood where I could see her reflection.

'Mum, do you need any help with tea?' I asked, keeping my voice low.

She shook her head. She never did after we'd fallen out or she'd had one of her mini meltdowns, as Grandad called them. I waited for a moment and cast an eye of contempt on the lit cigarette smoking away in a dish near the stove.

'You can set the table for five. Tina and Peter will be joining us,' she finally said.

'Why are—' I started, but she breathed through her nose loudly and slammed down the vegetable peeler before gripping on to the counter.

'Never mind…' I muttered.

I set the table while wondering why they were visiting on a Tuesday when they usually only came for Sunday dinner.

How unusual.

Though it had been an unusual day.

As I lay the final knife, I went back to the kitchen. Mum was leaning against the counter now, eyes on the bubbling mince, wine glass in hand. I was at least pleased to see the cigarette had been extinguished; I could always taste the smoke in the food. She didn't acknowledge me as I skirted around her to get to the side door where I left into the garden and walked around the side of the house to Fred's cottage.

I often went to his house after I'd fallen out with Mum, or for a change of scenery. Fred tended our plants and cut the grass. He'd been one of Dad's old school friends and came to live here not long before Nana B and Dad died. He used to work at the pit, but an accident left him unable to do his job.

Grandad allowed him to stay in the cottage for free as long as he did it up and tended the gardens. No one had lived in the cottage for around fifty years, but it was lovely now. It had rustic-looking bricks and a slate roof. Fred had painted the doors, window frames, and sills in gleaming white. He had also fastened a trellis to the brickwork so he could keep the climbing ivy under control. You'd never have known it had been almost derelict for a time.

I used the secret knock we'd come up with, and he promptly answered the door.

'What's happening, little fella?' he said. He always called me that, even though I'd grown up now. It did make me laugh sometimes.

I stared at his slippers as I asked, 'Can I come in for a bit? I'm staying out of Mum's way until tea's ready.'

'Sure thing, mate.' He moved aside, venturing deeper into his home so I could come in. I closed the door behind me as I entered. 'Sit yoursen down. Cuppa tea?' Fred asked from the kitchen.

'If you're having one, I will,' I replied as I sank onto his old settee.

'Aye, why not? I'm parched, had a busy day today. Planted Mrs Kelly's seeds for her. Must have done over a thousand of the little blighters,' he said while he filled the kettle and pulled out some cups and saucers.

I couldn't look at Fred while he spoke to me—not enough mirrors—so I kept my eyes on the far wall. He didn't provide for my needs like my family did, said he wasn't going to pander to me, but he liked me all the same whether I looked at him or not. This meant I only really knew what he looked like from the back and the side. He had blond hair, always wore a white t-shirt under his blue overalls, and wellies while outside and slippers when inside.

'Did you know Mum calls her Mrs Nosey-Nelly?'

'Oh, I know, JC. She took great pride in telling me about your ride home with PC Williams. Any sugar?' he asked.

'Two, please. I fell out with mum over it. Mrs Kelly rang her up and told her everything. I wasn't even doing anything, really.'

'I know that isn't true,' Fred said, bringing over two cups of tea. He didn't have any mugs, said tea should only ever be served in a cup.

'What do you mean?' I asked.

'Police don't take people home for no reason.'

I rolled my eyes. 'That's what mum said.'

Fred slurped at his tea. 'So, what did you do? Fighting, shoplifting… You know your dad would be extremely disappointed, JC.'

'No!' I lowered my cup from my mouth. 'Nothing like that. I was just following someone down the estate.'

'I see. Well, you know my feelings on the matter. At least you ain't following women, anymore. That's something.'

'I guess…' I shrugged.

'Did your mam smash one of your mirrors again?'

I hummed. 'Two this time. I'll replace them tomorrow and have them up in no time.'

'Good man. What's broken can always be replaced.'

Fred didn't agree with my hobbies. Though, the way I was feeling right now, I felt less inclined to follow anyone at all. Maybe I'd stop until I'd solved the shop mystery. I stared into my cup of tea. I had to share my worries about Mr Phillips, and I knew Fred could be trusted not to tell anyone. He never revealed anything I confided with him.

'Fred?'

'Yes, JC.'

'Something odd is going on in Claude's Antiques,' I said.

'What do you mean *odd*?'

'Mr Phillips has been acting weird for weeks now. Ever since he did a house clearance at that big house. Having secret meetings, forgetting to lock up, checking on his safe all the time…'

'Has he now?' Fred leaned forward, resting his forearms on his thighs. 'Have you asked him about it?'

'Sort of, but he says I needn't worry,' I said, putting my cup down to fold my arms. 'No one tells me anything.' I slumped back in the seat.

'Oh, JC, sure they do. As he said, he just doesn't want you to worry, that's all.'

I rolled my eyes again. Why shouldn't I worry about things? I wasn't a kid anymore.

'Anyway, I might know what it is,' he added.

'You do?' I said almost leaping from my seat.

'Well, I overheard Mrs Kelly telling her neighbour that some family members are trying to get something back Claude bought in that house clearance. Apparently, they objected to the sale. They're demanding its return, but Claude bought it fair and square.'

'Oh, do you really think that's what it could be?' I asked.

'Possibly, but we have to consider the source of the information here. Most of the time, Mrs Kelly is spreading gossip that isn't true. Don't worry, kid. If Claude feels you need to know what's happening, I'm sure he'll tell you. Now, hurry and drink up before your mam calls you back for your tea.'

I nodded and picked up my cup again. 'Tina and Pete are coming round tonight. It's unusual. They normally only come round on Sundays, but it's Tuesday today.'

'Happens,' Fred said mid-slurp. 'They've got something to tell you.'

I frowned and turned my head to look at Fred's knees. 'Like what?'

He laughed. 'How would I know? I'm just guessing lad.'

I sighed and relaxed with my cup in silence, wondering what Tina and Pete might have to share with us. But more importantly, now I had this new information about Mr Phillips to contend with too. Surely if he'd bought something, he had the right to do with it as he pleased. He wouldn't return anything for free, that I was certain of. Though I had to wonder what it was they so desperately wanted back.

CHAPTER SIX

THE FOUR OF US sat around the table in the dining room, eagerly awaiting whatever Mum had prepared for tea. She was a good cook. Even when we couldn't afford much, she always managed to prepare a delicious meal. Cooking was the only nice thing she did for the family.

There were fifteen mirrors in the dining room to make sure I had every angle of the room and table covered. We'd only started eating at the table after Dad died. Grandad insisted on it, said it would bring us closer as a family. We were never able to sit at the table when Dad was alive. He used it as a dumping ground for car and scooter parts; the pile always seemed to breed and get bigger overnight.

Grandad drummed his fingers lightly on the table until Tina broke the silence.

'How's work, my little magpie?' she asked me. Magpie was her childhood nickname for me. She still used it from time to time, even though she knew I didn't like it anymore.

I tutted. 'Do you have to call me that?' I whispered to her. 'It's embarrassing.'

She laughed. 'To who? There's nothing to be embarrassed about, John-Michael. You will always be my little magpie,' she said, ruffling my hair.

I smiled at her, then straightened my hair. Tina had always taken better care of me than Mum had, and I didn't mind admitting it. I think if you asked Mum, she would probably admit it too.

'Well, to answer your question, work is great,' I told her. I didn't want to share my concerns about Mr Phillips with her just yet—at least until I'd found out more. 'Mr Phillips is allowing me to repair mantel clocks now.'

Tina's reflection beamed. 'That's wonderful, JC! You'll be running the place in no time.' She chuckled, but I frowned, though before I could respond, Mum walked in carrying her best casserole dish between her flowered oven mittens and placed it in the centre of the table. She removed the lid to reveal a shepherd's pie sprinkled with cheese. Then she went and fetched a side of peas and carrots and a huge jug of thick, meaty gravy.

'This looks champion, Mrs Chester,' said Pete.

She chuckled. 'How many more times do I have to tell you? Call me Anna.'

'Sorry. Yes, of course, Anna,' he said.

Everybody filled their plates high with the pie and vegetables. I took the mash off my shepherd's pie to make a barrier between the peas and the mince. I hated peas or beans to touch my meat or fish. When Pete helped himself to a second serving, Mum went to get another bottle of wine to share around.

'You've barely touched your wine,' Mum said to my sister as she topped up Pete's glass. 'Something wrong, love?'

Mum never called me *love*. Tina had always been her favourite. I never resented Tina for it, though. Mum's actions weren't my sister's burdens to bear.

'Well, as a matter of fact, we have something to tell you,' Tina said, taking Pete's hand, forcing him to set down his knife and fork. I followed his actions and set mine down too.

Mum took a big gulp of her wine, as though it would prepare her for Tina's revelation. 'What is it?'

'Well'—her face broke into a huge smile that matched the one on her husband's face—'we are expecting.'

Mum squealed and almost knocked over her wine, Grandad clapped his hands, then got up and moved around the table to slap Pete on his back, and I sat wondering why my sister hadn't finished her sentence.

'Tina?' I said and waved in the mirror to get her attention. 'Tina!' I repeated louder when she didn't answer me.

Her eyes found my reflection. 'Yes, John-Michael, what is it?'

'I'm confused. What are you expecting and when?'

She laughed.

'A baby, John-Michael,' Mum interrupted. 'What did you think she was expecting, a nosebleed?'

'Mum!' Tina snapped.

'Well, why does he have to be such a simpleton?' Mum snorted as she topped up her glass. 'He should engage his brain once in a while.'

I picked up my fork and pushed around what was left on my plate while I chewed on my lip. It was looking like another argument was about to take place.

'He's not a simpleton, Mother. He's quite smart, he just takes what's being said as literal sometimes, that's all. God, I thought you'd have figured that one out by now,' she said, placing a protective hand over her belly.

'I'm going to be a great-grandpa,' Grandad finally spoke. 'I can't believe it! This is the best news I've heard all year. When's the little mite due, Tina, love?'

'October, November time. We think I'm around twelve weeks.'

'That's fantastic news, isn't it, Anna?'

I looked up at Mum's reflection. She sat with a scowl on her face. When would she stop with the comments and nastiness? She always knew how to spoil a perfectly good evening. Despite how close I was with my sister, I liked it better when Tina and Peter weren't here. When we would sit and eat in silence.

'Anna?' Grandad repeated.

'Yes, it's fantastic. Who would have thought it, aye? Me, a grandmother and still in my forties. I'm happy, Tina, I really am —for both of you.'

'Thanks, Mum.'

'Right, now don't be expecting me to start having my hair in curlers all the time or having one of them purple rinses. And it will be Nana. None of this *Grandma* business. I'm too young for that.'

Everyone chuckled except for me.

'If you say so, Mum.' Tina said, then turned to me. 'What do you think, John-Michael? You're going to be an uncle!'

'I am,' I said, allowing a grin to emerge on my face.

'You sure are, kid,' she said. 'And I'll tell you something, you're going to be the best uncle this town has ever seen.'

'That's right, I am. Can I take him to the park?' I asked eagerly.

'You betcha. When the baby is old enough, he *or she* will love their uncle to push them on the swings.'

'I think it's a boy,' I said.

'You do?' Tina laughed. 'So does Pete.'

'He does?' I asked, looking at Pete's reflection nodding back at me. Pete had settled well into our family; he accepted me and never once showed any distaste for the mirrors like all of Tina's previous boyfriends. I can't be sure, but I think it's why she married him.

'Great! I can't wait,' I added.

Grandad brought his knife and fork together with a clatter. 'Well, how about we get all these plates shifted and have a glass of the good stuff to celebrate?'

'I'll do it, Grandad,' I said, eager to get back into his good books. I swiftly stood and collected all the plates, cutlery, and serving dishes and took them into the kitchen, then came back with a bottle of *Famous Grouse* and four glass tumblers on a silver serving tray.

'Thanks, John-Michael,' Grandad said as I set it down.

'Just a smidge for me, Grandad,' Tina told him as he poured. 'Can't be drinking too much now I'm in the family way.'

'Pfft… Never did you two any harm when I drank and smoked—'cept maybe soft lad, over there.' Mum pointed a bony finger at me.

'Mother!' Tina banged her fist on the table. 'Will you quit it with the jabs and jibes on our John-Michael?' she said, her voice starting to rise. 'And I hope you didn't drink when you were pregnant with me. You were sixteen, for goodness' sake.'

'Easy, Tina, love,' Pete said softly. 'Stress isn't good for the baby.'

'Oh, shush, Pete, will ya! You've read one baby book in your lunch break and all of a sudden you're a pregnancy expert.'

Pete stared into his glass of whiskey, and I wondered if I should borrow a book on babies from the library. I'd be nearby tomorrow to buy new mirrors, anyway, so I may as well make use of my lending card too.

'If you don't quit it with your nastiness, Mum, I'm not sure I want you to be involved in any part of this baby's life,' Tina said, stroking her belly again.

'Yes, Anna, what were we talking about earlier?' Grandad snapped.

I hadn't heard the rest of their conversation after Mum's mini meltdown, so I had no idea what the remark meant.

Mum pouted. 'But—'

'But nothing. I want this kid to be surrounded by nothing but love and kindness. That goes for you all,' Tina said, eyeing everyone around the table. I froze for a moment, wondering if she was about to call Mum out on how she'd treated me over the years. She didn't, but it didn't matter. On the inside, I was glowing. I loved Tina; she always stuck up for me and took my side even though she didn't live with us, anymore.

'Right, enough with this talk,' said Grandad. 'Time for a toast. Do you want to do the honours, Pete?'

'That's alright, Stephen, you do it. I'm not much for words. Don't you remember the hash I made of my speech at our wedding?'

'Ha! Oh yeah, a good laugh that was.' Everyone chuckled around the table, but I just smiled. 'Here's to the both of you and the new addition. I know you're going to make fantastic parents, and I'm beyond proud to be a great-grandad to this new bairn. Cheers.' He raised his glass.

The four of them clinked their drinks and exchanged a few words, and I snuck away from the table to wash the pots and clear everything away in the kitchen. I'd just dipped my hands into the hot, soapy water when Tina appeared beside me. I knew it was her straight away. I knew her footsteps, and she wore a different scent to mum. Tina always smelled fresh and fruity, whereas Mum smelled like musk in the morning, then wine, mints, and cigarette smoke by the evening. I looked at our reflections in the window in front of me, and Tina smiled.

'We haven't had much time to speak tonight, JC. Are you sure everything is good with you? You've been a bit quiet,' she said.

'I'm alright, Tina, honestly. Just'—I stacked another clean plate on the drainer—'you know with Mum it can be a struggle sometimes.'

'Aye, I know. Don't you worry about her. In fact, ignore her when she's having one of her moments. She doesn't know what she's talking about most of the time. You carry on being your lovely self and leave Mum to me,' she said, patting me on the shoulder.

I took another plate and dunked it into the water as I chewed on the inside of my cheek. 'Umm… There's something I need to tell you.'

'What?' She turned her body closer to mine.

'PC Williams brought me home this morning… in a police car.'

'Oh,' was the only response from her mouth. Tina never judged me.

'I'd been following someone down the estate, and he caught me.'

'I see. Well, you weren't hurting anybody or causing trouble. He should stick to solving crimes, not giving you a ride home.'

'I agree,' I said, turning on the tap to top up the hot water.

'Is there anything else you want to talk about?' she asked. 'Mum, the baby, or work?'

She could always tell when things were sitting heavy in my mind.

I paused for a moment, placing a clean plate beside the others on the rack before replying. 'I heard Grandad and Mum arguing about me today. She hates me,' I whispered, then slammed a pan into the sink, sending soapy water across our reflections in the window.

Tina immediately reached for a tea towel to mop up the splash. 'She doesn't hate you, don't ever say that again.'

'She does, though. She said I took all her dreams away.' I chewed on my cheek again.

'Oh, JC, she doesn't mean it. Mum doesn't understand you, that's all. It's hard for her, seeing you every day. You look so much like Dad.'

'People keep saying that, but I don't think that's it. She says I'm trapped in my own world of mirrors and reflections.'

'I see,' she said, chucking the damp tea towel onto the worktop. 'Well, I guess there's no harm in telling you more. Mum isn't entirely blameless in all of this. In my opinion, she's partly the reason you are the way you are. Mum knows she has her faults, and she blames herself. Instead of facing the problems and trying to help you, she drinks them away and avoids you.'

I sighed. 'I don't want to be trapped, Tina. I want to be like everyone else.'

'You're unique, JC. Nothing wrong with that. If you want to be like others, it's your decision. To me, you're fine the way you are. However, if you need help coming up with a way forward, tell me. But don't do it for Mum or other people—do it for you. Do you hear me, JC?'

'Okay. I hear you.'

'Me and Pete are going now, and I'll see you Sunday, my little magpie. How do you feel about a hug today?'

'A little one,' I said. I wasn't too keen on affection. I felt better about it if I was the one who initiated it. Tina knew how I felt and kept it short.

'See you later, alligator.'

'In a while, crocodile,' I replied as I watched her walk away in the window.

CHAPTER SEVEN

I CLEANED AND SCRUBBED the kitchen until it sparkled. Everything was perfect and back in its place—the way I liked it. I checked my watch to find it was nearly nine o'clock. I'd been cleaning for almost two hours. So, I grabbed a nearby duster and made my way to bed, making sure to check every mirror I passed for any smears or dust.

As I lay in bed, the day's events replayed in my mind like a black-and-white movie. First, I thought about Mr Phillips and the secrets he was keeping. But most of all, I thought long and hard about the baby's arrival and the conversation I'd had with Tina.

I'd been brought home in a police car three times now, and I had no intention of increasing that number anytime soon. I figured there would be no harm if I kept my head up a bit more. I couldn't very well push the baby to the park if I didn't watch out for all the dangers that could befall him. Plus, I didn't want to be trapped in my own world any longer. I wanted to look at people —for me, not anyone else. Perhaps I could gradually phase it in. It would be hard, but I could try. Maybe not now, but in the coming weeks, once I'd dealt with other matters.

I also needed to increase my search efforts if I was going to find The One. I would follow a few more men who I would have probably passed on before now. Attempts had to be doubled, and I would start first thing in the morning after I'd been to the library and found a book on babies. If I was going to be an uncle, I wanted to be the best one.

➤➤➤ ◄◄◄

I didn't know what time I fell asleep, but I slept right through 'til five a.m.. I couldn't recall the last time I'd slept so long. I jumped out of bed, and when I looked in the mirror, a huge smile reflected back at me.

Complete happiness had swept over me in the night for the first time in years. It wasn't as though I'd been unhappy until now, it was only that things hadn't changed around here for years. I'd been stuck in a circle of cleaning, following, and working. Somehow, the news of the baby and the mystery in the shop had given me something else to think about, and that only filled me with happiness. Who'd have thought something so trivial could do that?

The joy made me decide to check on what Grandad had been tinkering with in the garage to see if I could help him out. I hadn't been in there for a while, what with work, cleaning, and searching for The One. I'd thought recently about starting with car mechanics again too. Maybe now was the ideal time.

I crept through the sleeping house, took Grandad's keys off the hook in the kitchen, and slipped outside. The sun hadn't risen yet, but it wouldn't be long before that particular star lit up the sky with her presence. Damp fog lingered around the house, patiently waiting for the golden ball in the sky to burn through its thin layer.

I gently pulled open the garage doors and fumbled for the light switch on the wall. My hand mingled with several cobwebs which I wiped off on my jeans before finally locating the switch. The bulb flickered a couple of times before staying on.

Straight away, I saw what he was working on. A Lambretta GP200 scooter lay on its side. It looked battered and worse for wear, like it had been stood in a shed or garage for a long time. The dirty, yellow side panel had been placed to the side and some other parts had been removed to reveal the flywheel, which still had a socket and ratchet attached to the nut. Spanners had been wedged in places like doorstops to prevent it from rotating. It looked like Grandad had been trying to take the flywheel off but hadn't been able to do it.

I knew he struggled with his hands these days. He said they hurt—especially in the cold weather—and when I had the chance to inspect them when he wasn't looking, I noticed they had become knobbly, as though extra bones had started to grow on the knuckles. His thin skin stretched over them like tissue paper, and he couldn't straighten his fingers anymore, which only made it more difficult to hold his tools.

I visualised in my mind what he'd been trying to accomplish. Each fin around the flywheel was grooved. I figured it was designed that way to catch the air to cool the cylinder as it turned to stop it from overheating. If the nut travelled in the same direction while it was running, it would come off. I knew then the nut had to be turned anticlockwise, and it appeared Grandad had been trying to turn it clockwise.

To get it off, I put one hand over the socket and ratchet, then grabbed a hammer to give the handle a knock. Before I tapped it, I paused. The back of my neck felt heavy, as if someone was watching me.

A sweet whistle.

I glanced over my shoulder to find a robin peering up at me from the ground just within the open garage door. It tilted its head, then flew back out the door. A vision of Dad swept through my mind with it. If he were alive now, it would have been him doing this task, and I'd be stood behind him, watching on. I'd come in here less and less since he died.

I looked back at the flywheel and hit the ratchet. It vibrated through my hand and the sound echoed around the garage, though it didn't budge. I hit it harder, and it immediately loosened, then I worked on taking it the rest of the way off.

When I examined it closer, I noticed it was threaded on the inside of the flywheel, so it must have needed an extractor. I scanned the tools on the floor that my Grandad had left out to see if I could do the next part.

'What's going on?!'

I toppled onto my backside with surprise and turned to see Grandad's slippered feet stood in the doorway; he'd clearly headed out here in a rush. His hand extended, and he leaned against the wall.

'I thought we were being robbed,' he sighed.

'Sorry, Grandad,' I said, getting up and brushing the dust off my jeans. 'I thought I'd see what you'd been doing and help you out.' There were no mirrors or many reflective surfaces in here, so I kept my eyes downcast on the grimy floor. He still had his dressing gown on, which looked more paisley-patterned smoking jacket, though he never smoked.

'Blimey, are you trying to finish me off, or what, lad?'

'I didn't mean to get you out of bed,' I said, twisting the ratchet I still had in my hand.

He exhaled slowly. 'Alright, not to worry, son. Now, shift out of the way. I want a gander at your handy work.'

I moved out of the way as he shuffled past me to inspect the scooter.

'You've got it off!' he exclaimed.

'Yes. I pictured it in my mind, like how I picture all the watch components to see how they work. I figured it had to turn anticlockwise, and you'd been trying to turn it clockwise,' I told him.

He slapped his hand against his forehead. 'Damn it. I should have remembered that. Not worked on one of these for a while. Only doing it as a favour for a mate, as he didn't know how to get it off and I thought I could do it. You've done a good job here, lad,' he said, his voice full of praise.

'Thanks. Do you want me to help you remove the rest?' I asked him.

'Nah, I'll handle it from here, son. You've done a grand job, though. Thanks.'

'You're welcome. How about I tidy up a bit for you?'

'Aye, you can do, lad. I'm off to get dressed, and I'll meet you back in the kitchen.'

Grandad lumbered off slowly. The happiness I'd woken up with remained, as he'd been glad of the help. The task had been easy too. I knew then I should start to help him out a bit more. After all, he wouldn't be able to take any handouts from Tina once she'd had the baby.

I straightened things up and put all the tools where they belonged. Grandad wasn't particularly good at making sure they were put away, said he couldn't find them again. Though I knew he only couldn't find them when he hadn't put them away, so I returned them all to the correct places in the system I'd created for him. Then I switched off the light, pulled the door to, and locked it up. You couldn't be too careful. Even though it was getting light, it didn't stop people from robbing you. Times were hard. Long gone were the days when you could trust your neighbours.

In the kitchen, I washed my hands with washing up liquid and sugar (the only mixture guaranteed to get grease off your hands), then scrubbed my nails with the nailbrush. I always liked to have clean hands; there was no excuse for dirty nails, no matter what job you had.

I filled the kettle and set it to boil. Just as it started to whistle, Grandad came down the hallway. It took him longer to get going in the morning these days.

'Cup of tea, Grandad?' I shouted.

'Yes, son, thank you,' he said as he sat at the table, slapping the morning's paper down with his glasses.

'You've really helped me out with that scooter.'

'I'm glad I could help. And I've put all your tools back where they belong,' I said, looking at his reflection. His eyes grew wide, then after a moment, his mouth pulled up into a grin.

'Have you really, lad?'

I nodded back at him.

'By heck, son, I hope I can find them all again.' He laughed. 'Especially with my hands the way they are now.'

I placed a mug of tea before him. 'It's really quite a simple system, Grandad, once you use it as I instructed.'

'Aye, suppose it is. Though it was years ago when you set that up. Probably not good having everything all over the floor at my age.'

I took a seat beside him and slurped at my tea before asking, 'Who does that scooter belong to? Do I know him?'

'No, I don't think so. He's just a bloke in town, down South Common. One of Keith's mates, Adi, said he couldn't find anyone free to do it. I said I'd give him a hand.'

'Oh right, good. I was thinking... Maybe if you wanted to start booking in a few jobs, I could do a few hours for you, get some more money coming in,' I said, watching his reflection as he stroked his chin for a moment.

'I couldn't ask you to do that, John-Michael. You've got a job and your... umm, hobbies.'

'You aren't asking me, Grandad, I'm asking you. I really want to help the family out, and I think if I help, things will improve around here for when the baby comes.'

'Who said things need improving?' he said, a quizzical look on his face.

'Well, I told myself. I woke up this morning with a new... outlook.'

'Does that mean you're going to stop following people?' he asked hesitantly.

He seemed to hold his breath as he waited for my answer.

'No, not yet,' I said, but continued at his deflated exhale, 'But I'm really going to try to stop, eventually. I can't very well take the baby to the park and follow people at the same time, can I? And do you know what else? One day, I hope to look at you all properly without the mirrors. Even mum,' I added.

'That's certainly something, John-Michael.' He paused to slurp more of his tea, then he tapped his fingers lightly on the table. 'I'll have to put the word out that we're taking on a few jobs, but I think I can get us a couple of services a week. What do you say?'

'I say great. Let me know when you need me, and I'll be ready.'

'Are you sure you can do this? I know how much you like to do… other things, JC.'

I nodded resolutely. 'I'm sure. In fact, I *want* to do this—for our family.'

'Well, then, I must say, John-Michael, you've well and truly surprised me this morning.' He drained his mug, then pulled the newspaper towards him. 'Right, I've got work to do and calls to make. How about you make us some toast with lashings of butter? Set us up for the day.'

I hadn't thought about eating until then. With all the excitement of my new outlook and the work I'd already done that morning, it had slipped my mind. I did as I was told, and as the smell of melted butter filled my nostrils, my stomach rumbled. I rammed down a slice before I got back to the table.

Ten minutes later, I cleaned up my plate and mug at the sink, then turned to Grandad's reflection; he was engrossed in the day's crossword.

'Water-clock…' he mumbled. 'Nine letters. What do you think, John-Michael?'

'Clepsydra,' I said. 'I'm going to get ready, Grandad. I need to go to the library.'

He raised an eyebrow, then scribbled down my answer. 'The library? You after any particular book? I thought you'd just about read every book on your favourite subjects in there.'

'Yes, I have, but I want a book on babies.'

'Babies?' He scoffed. 'Whatever for?'

'I want to learn about them before Tina's comes.'

'You are certainly taking your role as uncle seriously, aren't you?'

'I am, Grandad. I'm going to be the best one this town has ever seen.'

He laughed. 'I'm glad to hear it, son.'

CHAPTER EIGHT

I GOT WASHED AND changed, then retrieved my tattered library card and the shoebox from under the bed where all my money was saved. I would have even more money in it if Mum would stop smashing my mirrors on a weekly basis. I put the small, orange card in my wallet with some money and headed into town.

As I walked, the fog evaporated, and it looked like another moderately mild day. I reminded myself to keep my head up as much as possible, except when someone was walking my way. I found it difficult at first. My head kept lowering, forcing my eyes to drift back to the grey pavement beneath my feet. I had to battle hard with my brain to stop it from practising its usual instincts.

It made me smile to view the town properly instead of through quick glances here and there. There were things I hadn't noticed before, and though I still averted my gaze when someone came close, I enjoyed the new perspective and crossed my fingers in the hope I'd be able to maintain it.

As I approached the library, I was beginning to win the battle with my brain, when I spotted The Suit sat on my second-favourite bench. My hands balled into fists at my sides; I hated he had the nerve to be there, in my place, especially with the way his presence made my body react on sight. I didn't know what it was about him or what he was up to, but he didn't sit right with me.

As I got closer to him, I noticed he had an apple in one hand and a knife in the other. Pocketknives weren't uncommon; Grandad had a swiss army knife, and so had my dad and Fred. But to have one a few feet away from the police station was risky. I hoped PC Williams would spot him and he'd be arrested. Then hopefully, he'd be removed from our town where he didn't belong.

I crossed the road and leant against a lamppost outside the library to wait. People walked past, and I tried to watch them properly instead of watching their reflections as I usually did. It wasn't easy. My eyes would keep drifting back to the library's windows, fearful someone would turn and look me in the eye. But I also wanted to keep an eye on The Suit and see him get hauled away by the Police.

When I was younger, I often came to the library to get books on watches, though they didn't have many. However, I would still come week after week to see if they had anything new on the topic. They seemed to cater to older ladies more than anyone else, from all the books bearing men with their shirts open and women in their arms.

I went straight to the index cards listing the numbers of the Dewey Decimal System. An old librarian had taught me how to use them, and it wasn't long before I located the number I needed and off I went to look in that section of the library.

There weren't many books available, only a small handful. They looked brand new, as though only a couple of people had borrowed them. I took two I liked the covers of and went to the desk to check them out.

I placed them on the counter along with my library card and rang the brass bell for the assistant's attention. I kept my eyes firmly on the desk as she appeared. I expected her to ask me questions about the books I'd selected, but she barely noticed the titles as she stamped on the return date.

'Thank you,' I said as she slid the books back over to me and grunted.

I paused as I exited and scanned the street left and right just to be certain The Suit was nowhere to be seen. A half-eaten apple was the only evidence he'd been sat there. Happy I'd managed to get the books without incident and he had vanished once again, I almost skipped to my favourite bench to get in place, ready to look for The One.

As I hurried along, the familiar ring of Tab Hunter's pushbike bell ding-dinged behind me. Tab Hunter wasn't the man's real name. I didn't think anyone knew his proper name. I'd never see anyone talk to him at all, actually. I just knew that's what everyone called him due to his peculiar habit of picking up cigarette ends. And that wasn't the only peculiar thing about Tab Hunter. As his brown trousers rose with each pedal, the whole world could see that he wore ladies' stockings underneath his trousers.

When I found my usual place, I traced my hands over the rough surface of the bench and noticed a new carving on one of the slats which said, "*Craig woz 'ere.*" I had no idea who Craig was. Most of the people's names written here had blank faces to me, though it was possible I could have followed half of them.

I sat watching and waiting but nothing was biting, so eventually, I took myself for a slow walk to Woolworths. I passed the outside market (it wasn't on today) and weaved in and out of the empty stalls.

Next door to Woolworths stood a shoe shop; it was old-fashioned and family-run, and they looked to be having a sale on. I looked in the window; they sold slip-on shoes, black-leather moccasins, and sandals. In the next town, which was much bigger than ours, they had a Ribena shoe shop, which was a chain. There, they had Union Jack Doc Martins, studded punk-rock boots, bowling shoes, and Pods.

For my twenty-first birthday, I'd asked for some blue Pods. I'd seen them in a window when I visited with Tina. When I opened my gift, Mum had got me blue Tracks instead. They were cheaper than Pods and didn't look that dissimilar. Anyway, they were comfortable enough, so I couldn't complain. But I would buy some Pods at some point, I would make sure of it.

I went into Woolworths and selected two small mirrors; I didn't take as much care as I normally would when I picked them out. I had better things to do today. I carried them to the counter with my books placed on top to balance everything.

'Alright, John-Michael?' said Mavis. I'd got to know most of the women who worked here. Mavis was one of the older members of staff. If I had to guess, I would say she was about fifty. I never asked, though. Grandad told me it was extremely rude to ask a lady her age.

'Morning, Mavis,' I said using the mirrors to look up at her smiling face.

She frowned down at them.

'Ooh, John-Michael, these aren't our best mirrors, are you sure you don't want to have another look?' she asked.

'I'm busy today. Thank you, no, it's okay. Haven't got much time to browse,' I told her reflection.

'Okay, if you're sure. I know how much you love your mirrors. And what else have you got here?' she said, looking at the books now.

'My sister is having a baby, so I borrowed these from the library,' I said as I retrieved them and tucked them under my armpit.

'Aww, isn't that grand, a new baby. How lovely. Well, let me ring these up for you.'

As she gave me my receipt, she said, 'You ain't gonna be able to carry these and them mirrors. Give us them books; I'll put them in a carrier bag for you.'

'Oh, umm… Thank you.' I handed them over, and she passed them back to me in the bag, so I was able to hold the two mirrors under one arm and carry the bag with my free hand to sit back at my favourite bench.

⤜⤜⤜⤜ ⤛⤛⤛⤛

Time ebbed away rapidly, and it was looking more than likely I would have to choose someone to follow at random, or just go home. At one o'clock, my watch beeped. I scanned around to look for a man, any man.

My eyes were drawn to the reflection of a young man swaggering by; he had a skinhead, wore a polo shirt but no jacket despite the mild weather, braces, jeans, and oxblood Doc Martins with yellow laces. His jeans were rolled up over his boots, and you could see the tops of his white socks. I debated rolling mine up, too, but decided against it. I'd look stupid with the shoes I had on.

I took a deep breath and left the bench. I almost had to run to catch up with him; his legs moved fast, as though he was already being followed by someone and was trying to get away.

I tried not to use reflections as much as I had in the past. Instead, I concentrated on a small cross tattooed on the back of his neck. He had various other tattoos down the backs of his arms, including a love heart with an arrow through it and a coat of armour.

I tracked him at a steady pace, though not easily. I had never followed anyone who walked as fast as he did or swung their arms about from side to side so viciously. We didn't have many skinheads in town; however, I had seen a whole horde of them in Doncaster, hanging around the big shopping centre, smoking, and mouthing off at people. The women's heads were shaved, too, but they kept a fringe at the front with long strands of hair over their ears and long from the napes of their necks down. I had no idea what the style was meant to represent.

I followed him until he went into the record shop. Normally, I wouldn't follow someone into a shop. Instead, I would linger outside, pretending to browse the items in the window until they either came out or someone else caught my eye. This time, I decided I may as well go in. I had nothing to lose.

Downstairs was a stationery shop and upstairs was the record shop. The stairs were to the left as you walked in; I heard him stomping his boots on them. The woman behind the counter muttered "Unbelievable…" and shook her head.

I climbed the stairs when I could no longer hear his footsteps pounding their way up. When I reached the top, I saw the owner stood behind the counter facing the records, which were set in such a way he could see if anyone was trying to steal one. He wore a floral shirt and a flat cap; an odd combination.

I scanned the shop left and right to see where The Skinhead had gone. He was stood to my left at the end of the aisle where the S's were, most likely browsing the Ska records. I wouldn't have thought him a lover of swing or soul. I walked the long way round to look at the records opposite him which were the end of the R's.

As I strolled around, I glanced up at the walls to view all the posters dotted about which I hadn't looked at before. A poster of a red Ferrari caught my eye. Pinned next to it was a chart poster for the week, plus numerous others of bands such as Duran Duran and Spandau Ballet. I'd only seen them before in *Smash Hits* and *NME*.

I arrived opposite The Skinhead, though I didn't sneak a peek. I wasn't ready for the next step yet, and there was nothing reflective around to glance at him with.

I could hear him flicking through the sleeves, then every so often he would pick one out. I set my carrier bag down between my feet and copied his actions, flicking through my own section, and when he picked one out, I did too. After I put the third record back, I carried on pretending to scan through them, but The Skinhead didn't make a sound.

'Oi, weirdo.'

I stopped. I knew he was talking to me. Who else would he be saying that to? I grabbed my bag, gripping it tightly, and repositioned the mirrors with my other arm as I shuffled down towards the P's, ignoring him.

'Oi, ya weirdo. Why won't you look at me?' he asked.

I had to leave, and sharpish. I couldn't go back the way I came round the stacks; it would take too long. There was nothing I could do except run past him.

I didn't look at him or the shop owner as I moved, but I sensed the heat from The Skinhead's eyes burning into me as I dashed past him to the foot of the stairs. I went down two at a time and exited the shop.

That was a close one, I told myself as I walked down the street, swinging my bag to calm my nerves. It had been a disaster, and I missed looking at reflections; without them, I lost what was going on around me. That had been the whole reason I never followed anyone into places. There were no guarantees of any reflective surfaces or mirrors for me to use.

I hurried along, keeping a keen eye on the reflections as I walked. I thought I heard footsteps approaching behind me, but I didn't dare look over my shoulder for fear of my eyes meeting another's. It was difficult to see anything in the shop windows to my right.

PC Williams's warning came alive in my head: 'You know, if you end up following any of them ruffians and they spot you, you'll be in for a kicking.'

The footsteps got louder and nearer. I never expected the constable to be right. I'd always tried to be so careful, and I'd taken a massive risk today, all because of the happiness that I'd let seep into my soul.

An incredible force struck the middle of my back. I went sprawling onto the pavement, and the mirrors under my arm smashed, sending shards everywhere. I lost the grip on my bag as The Skinhead started kicking me. I curled into a ball, covered my head with my arms, and waited. It couldn't have lasted more than ten seconds, as people started yelling around me. He only managed to get three decent kicks in.

'Don't let me catch you near me again, ya weirdo,' he snarled, then spat. Thankfully, it didn't land on me. I peeked out through my fingers, spying his back retreating through the crowd that had gathered.

'You alright?' a man's voice said. I ignored him. I had to get my books back.

A hand touched me, and I flinched.

'Take it easy,' a woman said.

People tried to talk to me. I wanted them to leave me alone. I pushed myself into a sitting position with my knees pulled up towards my chin and my head tucked between them. I clasped my hands over my ears and squeezed my eyes closed, praying they would go away.

'Arr, leave him,' a man's muffled voice said. 'He's that weird Chester boy.'

After a few minutes, the crowd dispersed, leaving only a couple of people lingering about.

'Where are they?' I whispered.

'They what, lad?' a man said.

'My books. Where are they?!' I started to shout.

'Calm down, son, they can't have gone far,' he said.

I crawled about on my hands and knees despite the glass covering the pavement until I found the bag in the gutter. I scooped it up and scrambled to my feet to run off in the opposite direction as fast as my legs would take me. I didn't stop until I reached the park. The fact I could run told me he couldn't have done much damage.

I ran around the duck pond towards the back of the park. I stopped at a bench and sat down to wipe the dust and glass shards from my jeans, placing the books safe next to me. My breathing came thick and fast, and sweat trickled down my face. I swiped my forehead with the back of my hand to wipe it away, but when I brought it down, it was smeared with blood, not sweat. He must have caught my head with the edge of his boot.

I took out my small cigarette case with the mirror in so I could locate the wound and dabbed at it with the back of my jacket sleeve. It was only a nick, but I put a plaster on it, anyway.

He'd got in a couple of good kicks to my ribs, though I doubted any were broken. At least I had no marks on my face.

Someone cleared their throat behind me. I froze for a second, thinking The Skinhead had come back for round two. I lifted the mirror in front of me. WPC Thompson was stood behind me in uniform, her arms folded across her chest.

'What's going on, John-Michael? I've just seen you running through the park like a banger's been shot up your arse,' she said.

'Nothing. Nothing's going on. I'm only sitting here,' I said breathlessly.

She stepped closer so I could no longer see her face in the mirror. 'Well, what's that, then?' she asked. I could feel her peering over me. 'Blood?'

'Umm… I tripped,' I told her; it technically wasn't a lie. I had fallen onto the pavement when he shoved me.

She snorted. 'Yeah, likely story.'

I used my mirror to look for her colleague. She appeared to be on the beat alone again. I was beginning to think that this supposed partner of the constable was a figment of everyone's imagination.

'I thought women weren't allowed to patrol on their own?' I said.

'We're not, but I can take care of myself,' she said, sitting down next to me. 'He's off…buying cigs. And don't change the subject.'

'Fine,' I sighed.

'Women aren't delicate flowers that need looking after, you know. PC Williams is… old school. He believes a woman should be barefoot and pregnant. It's taken him a while to get used to women no longer being segregated. Anyway, I can take care of myself when I need to. I'll tell you a story about me, John, if you like? Can I call you John?' she asked.

'I prefer John-Michael. That's my name,' I told her.

'Fair enough. John-Michael, it is. When I was younger, younger than you are now'—she started to tell her story even though I hadn't given her an answer—'I used to live on the council estate. One day, this new family moved in from out of the area, and the kids were always looking for trouble. The talk on the streets was that the lass from the family wanted to have a scrap with me. She'd heard I was the hardest lass on the estate. That's the reputation you get from having brothers,' she said, gently nudging me with her shoulder. I slid a little away from her. If she noticed, she didn't mention it. 'You still with me?' she asked.

'Yes,' I nodded.

'I stayed out of her way as long as I could, until one day she confronted me. I tried to walk away, but she kept pulling at my hair—hard.'

'My sister said girls pull hair when they fight,' I said.

WPC Thompson hummed. 'Most do, but not me. No, I went into that fight like a lad with my fists punching and my legs kicking. In the end, my brothers had to pull me off her. And you know what? She never came near me again. So, you see, John-Michael, I don't need anyone looking out for me.'

I closed my eyes and thought about WPC Thompson's story as I listened to the sounds in the park. A gentle breeze rustled the trees and the shouts and screams of children playing nearby invoked a long-forgotten memory in me. 'That happened to me once,' I told her.

'Why? What happened to you?'

'My sensei had to take me off someone once—at karate,' I said, shuffling my shoes on the loose dirt beneath them. 'I started hitting my sparring partner, and once I started, I couldn't stop. He said everyone was yelling at me to quit. I didn't hear them. I wasn't allowed to go anymore after that.'

'Hmm, I see. Why didn't you hear them telling you to stop?'

'I don't know.' I moved my gaze to the overcast sky. 'I used to get focused on one thing and everything else going on around me shut off. I'm better now.'

'I'm glad you've worked that out, John-Michael.'

'Thank you, umm, ma'am...' I said. I couldn't very well say sir, could I? She'd probably clip me around the head.

But she laughed. 'Ma'am? Ooh, hark at you with the niceties. Officer Thompson will do.'

'Okay, Officer Thompson. Can I go now?'

'Not yet. Now I've shared something about myself, I think it's only fair that you tell me what happened to you and why you were running through the park like Carl Lewis.'

'I can't tell you.'

'You will have to tell me something, John-Michael, or do I need to fetch PC Williams to take you home again?' she said. 'You know he won't be happy taking you home twice in one week.' She made to get up.

I sighed. 'Okay, I'll tell you. Just don't tell PC Williams, please. He'll tell my grandad,' I said as I pushed my palms together into an almost-praying position.

'Deal,' she said.

'This lad beat me up,' I told her.

'If you know karate, why didn't you defend yourself?'

I shrugged. 'Sensei said you can't use it outside the dojo. Plus, I can't remember much. It was a long time ago.'

'You should always try to defend yourself. Nothing wrong with that,' she told me. 'Anyway, back to what happened. What lad? And why?' She had a suspicious tone to her voice that I was all too familiar with from Mum.

I crossed my arms but winced when I pressed on a bruised rib, so I held my hands on my lap instead. 'I wasn't doing anything. I was only browsing albums in the record shop, and this lad called me a weirdo. I left, and the next minute, he's kicking me in the street,' I said, my eyes focused on the dried blood on the back of my hand that I'd forgotten up to wipe off. I licked my finger and rubbed it away.

'I see…' Officer Thompson pondered. 'And what were you doing before you went into the record shop? Did you happen to be following this lad you mentioned?'

'Well, yes… But he hadn't noticed me, and I never did anything to him,' I added quickly.

'You've been told not to follow people, haven't you, John-Michael?'

I nodded. I knew that. I'd lost count of the number of times I'd been told what I was doing was wrong.

'In any case, that doesn't mean you deserved to be beaten up over it. He could have just told you to clear off. That's what I'd have done.'

She drummed her fingers on the bench and didn't speak for several minutes. I looked up slightly and observed the park. There weren't many people here, just a couple of mums pushing their kids on the swings and several others throwing balls and frisbees to their dogs. It was still mild out, but in a few weeks, the weather would be warmer, and the park would get much busier.

'Here's what we're going to do, John-Michael. You're going to tell me what this rogue looks like, then we're going to go find him and have a word,' she said.

I chewed on my lip and shook my head. What if it made him angry, and he tried to find me and beat me up again, or worse? Bring his friends along too.

'No, I don't think so. I'm not allowed. Mum said I shouldn't tell tales.'

'Okay. Well, why don't you walk back with me through town, and I'll make sure you're safe. We can see where PC Skive-a-lot has got to. I'm due back soon, anyway.'

I pursed my lips. It *would* be nice to have some protection as I walked back just in case I should bump into him again. So, I nodded and picked up my books, tucking the bag under my arm as we made to leave.

'What's them books you've got?' Officer Thompson asked as we walked.

'Books on babies,' I said. 'My sister is having a baby soon, and I want to learn all I can about them.'

'Well, isn't that something.' She chuckled. 'You'll make a mighty fine uncle.'

'Thank you.' I smiled, and we continued on in silence.

We started walking not long before we got to town, she questioned me again.

'Did this lad have any tattoos?' she asked. 'These lads around here all look the same with their stupid outfits, don't you think John-Michael?'

'No, they're not all the same. Everyone has subtle differences I notice them all when I'm watching or following people.'

'Oh, is that right? Like what?'

'Different buttons, laces, tattoos, hair, the way they walk, the way they stand, all sorts.'

'You notice these little things, do you? Why are you following these people? It can't be just to see what they look like and what they are wearing, can it?'

'I'm looking for something?'

'What fashion crimes?' she laughed.

'I don't know yet,' I whispered.

Why did everyone always ask me that? I was just about sick of it.

'Well, you must be able to give me an accurate description then?'

'I could yes. But I'm not allowed, mum said.'

'Yes, I know what your mam said, but I'm the police and I outrank your mam.'

'You do?' I asked her.

'Of course, I do. Now, are you going to tell me?'

'Okay I nicknamed him The Skinhead,' I told her.

'Great, well that doesn't exactly narrow it down they do look the same as each other,' she sighed.

'Yes, sort of, but they don't all have tattoos on the back of their necks,' I said.

'No, they've got them on their hands and their faces and everywhere. I've seen kids draw better pictures then what they've got tattooed.'

I laughed at her comparison.

'Wow, hold on did you just laugh? I don't think I've heard you laugh before John-Michael.'

I bit my lip. I never laughed often, had nothing much to laugh at before.

We were back in town now, near the shops I wanted to go home through the orchard to avoid it, but she told me not to be scared and we should go straight past the shops. I reluctantly agreed, as we got near the jewellers, we spotted four skinheads, she turned to face me, and I looked down.

'Right, you just wait here a minute, look in the shop window or something,' she told me.

WPC Thompson walked towards them exaggerating her swagger trying to make herself look bigger than she actually was.

'Oi, you four, stop where you are,' she yelled.

I looked at the group expecting them all to run off when they spotted her, instead, they started scuffling amongst themselves trying to pass a small bag onto the other. The skinny one of the group ended up with the bag and he was pushed to the floor in the commotion as the other three scattered in different directions. He also happened to be the kid who had kicked me earlier. She grabbed him by his collar and twisted it round in her hand it looked as though she was choking him.

'What's this?' she yelled and grabbed whatever he had in his hand. She reached for her handcuffs and pulled his arms behind his back, cuffed him then dragged him to his feet. He staggered as he got up and they almost went down together in a heap.

'It's not mine, 'e dropped it,' he said as she inspected the package and pulled out a tobacco tin.

'You're coming to the police station with me,' she said after examining its contents.

'I told you it's not mine. It were Rob, Frankie and Mick's,' he whined.

'Well, they're not here now are they, you little squealer,' she shouted for the gathering crowd to hear.

She pushed him towards the direction of the police station, then paused, she turned slightly to the side and gave a sort of wave even though she had her hands full. I made the rest of the way home on my own.

CHAPTER NINE

AT HOME, I DISAPPEARED into my bedroom. I removed my jacket and hid it in my laundry pile, wondering if I'd be able to get blood out of the denim. Then I went to the mirror to check my head, gently peeling back the plaster. The cut had stopped bleeding, and with the way my hair fell, you would barely notice it.

I lifted up my T-shirt and checked my chest and stomach. I had a red mark on my side, but no serious damage, and it only hurt if I pressed down on it. I had come away fairly unscathed for my first fight. Though I guess I couldn't really call it a fight, since I didn't take part.

I slumped onto my bed, and a mixture of relief and anxiety washed over me. Everybody had warned me this would happen, but I'd refused to believe them. What would I do now? How would I know who was safe to follow and who wasn't? The beating had shaken my confidence. Could I potentially fall victim to those I followed? Would I have to stop now? So many questions whirled through my head, making my temples thud and ache at the same time.

For now, I would have to stop all my efforts until I could figure out what to do next. Though the thought only filled me with dread and made my stomach knot. The happiness I'd felt this morning had evaporated with a quick blow to the ribs. I'd followed people for as long as I could remember. When I was little, I would be at my mother's side one minute and gone the next, padding off after some stranger down the street. And now it felt as though I had to stop all I knew. I had wanted to stop, yes, but in my own time. Not because of my own stupid mistake.

I didn't move from my bed, not even when Grandad knocked on my door asking if I wanted supper, as I hadn't been down for tea. He told me he'd booked in a couple of services for Friday. I'd told him that was great as enthusiastically as I could, and I heard him harrumph and shuffle back down the hall.

I didn't sleep well, only nodding off here and there, getting less sleep than I was used to. I tried reading the baby books I'd borrowed from the library to drift off again, but they didn't help much, either, and there were parts I didn't understand.

To take my mind off the thudding in my head and the twisting in my stomach, I dusted the mirrors in my room, then decided to reorganise my music records. I currently had them in alphabetical order by genre, and by my favourite ones in that genre. I took them all off the shelf, wiped them down, then proceeded to sort them into alphabetical order by the artist's name.

By the time I was done, the sun was rising, and I could only wonder if what I was looking for in the people I followed wasn't real. What if it was just something I'd thought up as a way to distract myself from the words Mum said to me all those years ago, for everything I was missing out on? What if Tina was right? What if I was perfect the way I was?

After my usual breakfast, I hurried to work, taking the shortcut through the orchard. I kept my head down, not looking at any reflections in shop windows. If I didn't have a job, I would have quite happily stayed in my room after breakfast with my head under the covers until my world was back to how I liked it. But deep down, I didn't think things would ever be the same again.

I froze in the middle of the pavement as I turned the corner. The Suit was coming out of Claude's Antiques, and the same horrible shiver ran from my toes to my scalp.

Crap! I thought. I'd forgotten all about him. I'd have to remember to include this sighting in my journal when I got home too. I hadn't included The Skinhead. I didn't want any lasting reminders of that disaster.

I watched The Suit as he tugged on the hem of his jacket before brushing the front of it with the back of his hands and repeating the same motion with his sleeves. He walked away with his shoulders back and arms swinging.

Suspicious, I walked through the door, and the bell rang.

Mr Phillips was missing from his usual spot.

I paused and took a step back; some items were out of place. Nothing missing, just off by a few centimetres. And drawers in some of the bureaus and sideboards hung open, like someone had been searching for something and not had the patience to shut them properly.

'Mr Phillips?' I called.

No reply.

I knew where every antique belonged in the shop. I had it all memorised. Any time a piece sold, I would remove it from the picture stored in my head. I wondered if Mr Phillips had lost something, or if The Suit had stolen something.

"Mr Phillips!" I shouted again.

Nothing.

I checked the till. Mr Phillips had taught me how to use it, though I'd only used it twice. The till still had money in it, so it was unlikely The Suit had robbed the place, and nothing appeared to be missing—except for Mr Phillips.

I hurried around the shop, straightening everything, and shutting the drawers, then walked through the passage, passing the locked door to the flat upstairs, to the kitchen and the back office. But he wasn't there.

I frowned. He had to be somewhere; he would never leave the shop unattended. I checked the back door, but it was locked from the inside.

A distant, muffled shuffle.

My head snapped up and rotated on my neck. The sound had come from the room where I worked.

I went straight there and stood in the doorway, scanning the area with narrowed eyes. Then a tuft of white hair drew my attention. I approached it and found Mr Phillips sat on the floor behind a wooden tea chest. His head hung almost on his chest, his usually slicked-down hair was out of place, and his shirt was dishevelled, like someone had grabbed him by it and twisted it in their hands.

'Mr Phillips?' I whispered.

Silence.

'Mr Phillips?' I said a bit louder, wondering if he was asleep, or worse.

But his head shot up. 'Who is it?!'

I averted my gaze quickly when his eyes found me. 'It's me, Mr Phillips. John-Michael.'

'John-Michael?'

'Yes, is everything alright? What happened?'

'Oh, John-Michael. Help me up, will you? I won't look you in the face,' he said.

'Sure, okay.' I said, even though I was clueless as to what had happened and why I had found him huddled in the corner. I felt uncomfortable touching him. I might have worked with him for eight years, but he wasn't family (and sometimes touching *them* could be a challenge).

I grabbed a duster and draped it over my hand, then helped Mr Phillips up and guided him to my chair. At least then I could see him in the mirrors.

I watched as he straightened his shirt and smoothed down his hair. I gave him a minute before I probed him again. His face looked pale and clammy. I couldn't decide whether to phone for a doctor or the police. He looked dazed, like he had seen a ghost. What could The Suit have possibly said to him?

So, I left him sitting and put the kettle on. I knew he kept a bottle of whiskey in the back of the cupboard, so I poured out a good measure (I knew it was good for shock), then I made two cups of sweet tea and brought them back on a round tray advertising Darley's Brewery. Mr Phillips hadn't moved from the position I'd left him in.

I set down the tray and handed him the whiskey first. He swallowed it down in one gulp, coughed and spluttered, then gave the glass back to me. I didn't know if he wanted a refill, as he didn't say anything, so I went and topped it up, anyway. He took the refilled glass from me but only took a sip this time and smacked his lips.

'Thanks,' he said, sounding a bit more like himself. 'I needed that, lad.'

'What happened?' I finally asked.

'Hand me that cup of tea,' he said, indicating with his head.

Realising Mr Phillips probably wasn't going to move from my seat anytime soon, I pulled over an old chair in need of upholstering so I could sit. I shuffled uncomfortably in the seat as a spring jabbed me in the backside, then I handed him his tea, which he took with a slightly trembling hand.

'If anything happens... to me,' he started to say, then cleared his throat. 'If something should happen to me,' he said again, 'I want you to know they are in the large safe. Don't let anyone get their hands on them. The key to the small safe is in the back of my pocket watch. All my important documents are in that safe; you'll be needing them. And the key to the bigger safe is in a small box in there too. You'll know how to get the key out, won't you, John-Michael?'

'Of course, Mr Phillips. But what's going to happen to you? And what's in the safe?' I asked him.

He turned his head slightly, and his forehead crinkled. 'Ay? Oh, nothing, lad. I think he's gone now.'

'Who's gone?' I asked. He didn't answer. Instead, he pulled out his handkerchief and wiped his forehead. The colour started to come back to his cheeks after a few sips of the sweet tea.

'We best get on, lad.' He got up and walked towards the door before turning to say, 'If it wasn't for you, I wouldn't be able to keep the shop running. You're a good lad, John-Michael.'

I was left to gawp at the back of his head, wondering what could have possibly happened to leave him in such a state. And what on earth was he keeping in the safe? Perhaps I needed to find out for myself.

⤜⤛ ⤜⤛

I kept an eye on Mr Phillips for the rest of the day in between doing my work. I noticed he jumped every time the doorbell rang—which thankfully wasn't often. I was desperate to find out what had taken place that morning, especially if it could affect me too. I couldn't ask him again, though; he obviously didn't want to tell me. If Mr Phillips was in trouble, I was going to have to find out how to help on my own.

About an hour after the incident, Mr Phillips's yells brought me running to the main shop. I was greeted by two schoolboys, still in their uniforms, prodding at the pendulum inside an old grandfather clock.

'Don't touch that, either,' Mr Phillips scolded them.

'Alright, mister, keep your hair on,' the smaller of the two said, and they both started laughing.

I approached the clock when they moved away from it, closing the door gently and wiping the glass of their greasy fingerprints.

'What do you want? Shouldn't you both be in school?' Mr Phillips said.

'We want two fishing nets, mister,' said the bigger kid.

'You want to be across the road at the hardware shop, not here,' he told them.

'Yeah, well, it's shut, ain't it? That's why we're here.'

The pair laughed again.

Mr Phillips grumbled and approached the counter. 'What're your names? I'm ringing the school.' He picked up the phone.

'Albert and Elsie,' the bigger one said as they ran out the door.

Mr Phillips slammed the handset down. 'Flaming kids,' he muttered under his breath.

'What do they want fishing nets for? They aren't old enough to fish, are they?' I asked.

He scoffed. 'They're only after tadpoles in the dykes. Didn't you ever go with your dad?' he asked, returning to his ledger.

I bit down on my lip. Dad had never taken me. He'd always been too ill.

'Oh, sorry, lad. I forgot for a moment then. I've not been with it lately. Forget I said anything.'

'Okay, Mr Phillips…' I turned to go back to my workstation, but his voice made me stop.

'John-Michael.'

I lifted my head to meet his stare in the mirror ahead of me.

'You know, Mary and I always said if we'd had a son, we'd have wanted him to be as nice as you. I know you'll do right by me and figure everything out,' he said.

The doorbell rang again, and Mr Phillips rolled his eyes. 'I thought I told you two we don't—' But as he turned, he staggered back, crashing into a cabinet, and knocking a pencil to the floor.

'Woah, you alright?' one of the customers said.

There were two of them, both male, but judging by the bemused look they gave Mr Phillips, I guessed they knew each other.

'Sorry, Clive… Fersy,' Mr Phillips said as he regained his composure and retrieved his pencil. 'What can I do for you two?'

I wanted to observe what they'd come in for, as the men were huge. The first man stood at over six feet, and the other was only slightly shorter. The bigger of the two carried a large, leather sports bag in his beefy hands.

I grabbed a pocket watch I'd finished earlier and a duster to clean it and stood in the rear doorway polishing it so I could listen to their conversation and view them in the mirrors.

'What have you got there, Clive?' Mr Phillips asked.

Clive heaved the bag onto the counter, and it landed with a thud. 'Take a peek.'

Mr Phillips put down his pencil, unzipped the bag, and peered inside. He looked back at the men, then back at whatever was in the bag, then he pulled his glasses down from his head to his nose to inspect it further.

'Is it a mace?' he asked.

'No, it's a flail,' Clive answered. 'A mace is a ball on a stick. A flail is a handle with a chain and a ball.' He pointed with his head. 'Knights used to swing 'em round and belt people with 'em.'

I stopped pretending to polish the watch and stared at the bag they had put on the counter. I almost bounced on the spot. I wanted to edge closer to examine it for myself, but thought better of it and stayed put.

I watched them in the mirror when a shift of movement on the wall beyond Mr Phillips moved my gaze aside. For a second, I swore I saw a dark figure there, concealed by the shadows in the corner. I glanced behind me quickly—nothing there—and back to the mirror.

'How old is it?' Mr Phillips asked, bringing my attention back to the new antique.

'We don't know.' They both shrugged. 'That's why we've come to see you. Thought you might know, or know someone who does.'

'Where'd you get it from?'

This time, the other bloke answered. 'Our Andrew swapped it for a Madness LP. A couple of lads found it down near the Foot Trods. The council were putting a new ditch in, and they found it there one afternoon after they'd left for the day.'

'Ya, what?' Mr Phillips scoffed. 'Your Andrew got this in exchange for some weird music? If you can even call what the kids listen to these days *music*...'

The pair chuckled.

'Is it genuine?' asked Clive.

'Possibly. Can I hang on to it for a couple of days to check it over?'

'Sure, why not?'

'You got a phone yet?' Mr Phillips asked.

Clive shook his head. 'I ain't getting one of them when there is a perfectly good phone box at the end of the road.'

'Fair enough. Right, can you come back for it on Saturday?'

'Aye,' he said, then they turned and left.

When the door shut behind them, I emerged from the back of the shop.

'Is it genuine?' I asked.

'Aye, it might just be, lad.'

'Can I have a look?' I asked his reflection.

Mr Phillips nodded, and I almost ran over to peer inside. I'd only ever seen them in history books, and who knows where Clive and Fersy had really got this one from—as if the council hadn't seen it and loaded it onto the back of their pick-up. I couldn't believe what I was looking at; it appeared to be real and old with all the dirt on it.

'Can I touch it?' I asked him.

'Yeah, go ahead,' he said.

I moved closer and placed my hand over it for a moment. When I finally touched it, the hairs on the back of my neck stood up and a shiver ran right through me.

'What was that lad?' asked Mr Phillips.

'I don't know, something made me shiver.'

'Maybe the former owner has dropped by to say hello.' He chuckled.

I really hoped they hadn't. I didn't know if I believed in ghosts and all that nonsense. But I had seen something lurking in the corner; perhaps Mr Phillips was right, and its former owner *had* appeared to watch over it.

Then I wondered what it was about The Suit that had evoked the same reaction in me.

CHAPTER TEN

I STAYED LATER THAN I normally would, feigning I still had work to do so I could make sure Mr Phillips was all right, which he seemed to be by the end of the day. He'd become engrossed by the flail, which I'd helped him to move (it was heavier than it looked). I wondered how knights were able to carry them with all their armour on and ride a horse at the same time.

On my way out, I reminded Mr Phillips to lock the door after me; he nodded he would.

Outside, I glanced over the road, spotting The Suit leaning on a lamppost, watching the shop. He saw me and smiled, but it wasn't a nice smile this time. It was creepy, and it made me shiver more than last time. He broke my gaze to look at his fingernails.

Tyres screeched, followed by a bang.

My eyes darted to where the commotion came from. A woman stood at the other side of the road, looking down the street with her hands clasped over her mouth. I followed her line of sight and spotted a car that had mounted the kerb. Farther down the road, a scooter lay with its front wheel still spinning. Its rider lay around four metres away from the bike. I glanced back to where The Suit had been standing, but he'd vanished. Again.

No one went over to the rider in the road. A couple of people stood and stared, while someone shouted that they were going to ring an ambulance. Everyone appeared to be in shock, but after a few seconds, they started to move. A woman ran over to check the occupant of the car; it appeared to me as though the car had pulled out on the scooter at the junction.

'It's not good,' I said out loud. I wracked my brain for what I'd seen on TV and how they dealt with accidents, but all that popped into my head, to begin with, were the *Carry On* films. I knew I had plasters in my pocket, though I didn't think they would help anyone here.

I searched my brain for something else, then remembered the TV series *Angels*. I knew then I had to talk to the rider, keep him awake, and make him comfortable.

I ran off towards him and stopped a little way off to see if I could see his face. He had an open-faced helmet on, mirrored sunglasses, and a scarf covering his mouth and nose. His leg twitched, and he groaned. I got down to him as fast as I could.

'My name is John-Michael,' I said looking at my own reflection in his mirrored sunglasses. He didn't answer.

I cast my eyes up and down his body; there didn't appear to be any injuries on the outside. Just a couple of grazes on his fingers. He groaned again, and his fingers trembled.

'Hello, what's your name?' I asked.

He didn't answer.

'Hello!' I repeated.

'Hi,' he groaned and tried to move.

'You need to stay still. Don't move and remain calm,' I told him.

'Okay,' he whispered.

'I think you're going to be alright. An ambulance is coming. I'm going to put a plaster on your finger. It's only a small graze,' I said, retrieving a plaster from my wallet.

He sighed heavily. 'I'm Daniel.'

'Hi, Daniel.'

'Come out of the way quick. I'm a first-aider!' someone shouted at me.

I moved to let the man look at Daniel. Then sirens could be heard coming round the corner, and up pulled a police car, its tyres screeching. I protected my ears until the sirens stopped.

PC Williams got out with another officer and began shouting instructions to bystanders and his colleague. He spotted me.

'Go home, John.'

'But I…'

'But nothing. Get yoursen off home. Now.'

I crossed my arms and turned my back on the carnage. 'I can't believe you're sending me home when I helped,' I muttered under my breath.

⋙ ⋘

'You've been awfully quiet,' said Grandad as we sat around the table for tea. 'Is something the matter?' he asked.

I hadn't spoken a word since PC Williams told me to get off home. Questions swirled around my head that I didn't understand, memories of my dad mixed with visions of the accident. I didn't know what my dad had to do with Daniel. I hoped it didn't mean he would die too. I couldn't conceive of the idea. And would it be my fault if he did?

'I witnessed something awful today,' I told him.

Mum slapped her hand on the table. 'Oh, here we go.'

Grandad ignored her, keeping his eyes on my reflection. 'What did you see, son?'

'Someone got knocked off their scooter, down near the shops.'

'Oh, gracious!' Grandad gasped, though his eyes flicked disapprovingly to Mum before returning to me. 'Were they alright?'

'I hope so. He looked alright on the outside. His name's Daniel.'

'You spoke to him?' asked Mum.

'Yeah. No one checked on him to start with. They were more interested in the driver of the car. I thought it best someone went over. It was okay, he had sunglasses on,' I told her. I was sure I saw a touch of a smile on her face. I hadn't seen her smile for so long, it was hard to tell if that's what it was.

'That was very brave of you, lad,' said Grandad.

'Do you think you could find out if he's alright? I'd like to know,' I said.

'Yeah, I'll call PC Williams after tea.'

'Thanks.'

I shuffled the fish fingers and chips around my plate, making sure they didn't go anywhere near the peas.

'Aren't you hungry?' asked Mum. There was a kindness in her voice I wasn't used to.

'Not really,' I told her.

'Why don't you go lie down, and I'll fetch you some sweet tea and a slice of apple pie. I think there's a bit left,' she said. 'I think that'll cheer you up a bit.'

I shared a surprised glance with Grandad. She hadn't been this way with me in a long time, if ever.

'That would be great,' I said before she had a chance to change her mind. Who knew when such a gesture would be offered again.

I went straight to my room, not even stopping to check if the mirrors were clean as I passed by and lay down on my bed to stare up at the ceiling. The pounding in my head remained. I hadn't been able to shake it away all day.

I looked at Bruce Lee on the poster and wondered what he would have done in my shoes. I couldn't shake the day's events from my mind. Something was wrong in Claude's Antiques, and I was determined to find out what it was. I needed my job. It gave me purpose. It wasn't just a means to buy and replace the mirrors Mum smashed.

A knock on the door brought me back to now.

'Yes?' I called out.

'Can I come in?' It was Mum's muffled voice.

'Sure,' I said, though I carried on staring at Bruce Lee.

'Here you go,' she said, putting a plate and mug on my bedside table. 'I've made it sweet for the shock,' she added. 'It can't have been nice to see that accident. It was mighty kind of you to go over to that man. I never thought you'd do something like that.'

'Thank you, Mum. I'm trying to be different. More helpful,' I said.

'Hmm, 'tis nice in here,' she said, not acknowledging my words. 'You've always been one for tidying up after yourself. Even when you were small, you put your toys away, and you do keep the house clean,' she said.

I didn't know what to say. I couldn't be certain if she was trying to thank me or give me a compliment.

'Umm… I do try,' I said.

'I know I can be hard on you sometimes… It's only because I just don't understand your ways, and I'm mad at myself. I feel like I'm responsible—like I did something wrong.' She sniffed. 'Well, I don't *feel* I did. I *know* I did…' She trailed off.

Wow, this is different, I thought.

'I don't think you've done anything wrong,' I told her. I swung my legs around and sat up. She was looking into one of my mirrors, and I blinked back at her. Her eyes had filled with tears. I knew she had said those things about my eyes all those years ago, but could she really be responsible for how I'd turned out?

I didn't think it mattered anymore, anyway. It seemed we were both turning a corner.

'I'm proud of you for trying to help that man today,' she said, then hurried out and closed the door before I had the chance to reply.

I gawked at the door. This was why I had to fight everything I'd come to know and love, stop with the following, and stop using the mirrors. If I went back to my old ways, then she probably would too.

I lay back down. 'What would you do, Bruce?' I asked the poster.

I knew his answer: Bruce would get to the bottom of the trouble Mr Phillips was having, while I watched on helpless. What could I do? Me, the weird kid who didn't look at people in the eye, who had to use mirrors to have a proper conversation. All because of a few choice words my mum had said to me years ago. Was that really the reason? Or was this just me?

I'd been through so much in two days; getting beaten up, helping Mr Phillips with his shock, then going through my own after witnessing the accident.

Then I sat bolt upright.

'The Suit,' I said out loud.

In the chaos, I'd forgotten about him—yet again. I grabbed my journal and wrote about the latest sightings of him. The only thing I was certain of was that he didn't belong in this town, or anywhere in Yorkshire, for that matter. No one really dressed like that here, plus the suit looked awfully expensive and tailormade. People that I knew of normally only wore suits for weddings and funerals—except Pete. He wore a suit, but the bank he worked at was in Leeds, and his attire wasn't as nice as The Suit's. I wished I'd had the opportunity to follow him. Perhaps then I could figure out who he was and what he wanted with Claude's antique shop.

I drank the tea and ate the pie mum had left me. I didn't taste it and only ate out of necessity. After writing in my journal, I didn't feel like doing anything else, not even cleaning my mirrors. I wanted to sleep to try to take the thud in my head away. However, every time I shut my eyes and drifted off, I saw the scooter with its wheel still spinning and Daniel hurt beside it.

I would walk over to look at him. His scarf and mirrored sunglasses had disappeared, and his eyes were open, staring up at me, making me want to turn and run. But my feet wouldn't budge. It was like they had sunk into the tarmac.

I shut my eyes and shouted for it all to go away, and when I opened them, that scene had vanished, replaced by The Suit. He was standing behind me in a mirror in Claude's Antiques as I looked in the big safe. He flashed a bright white smile, then winked.

I jumped into wakefulness at a light tapping on my bedroom door.

'Yeah,' I croaked. I checked my watch. It was eleven p.m., though it felt much later.

'Can I come in?' asked Grandad.

'Yes,' I said, sitting up. I watched him in the mirror. His mouth sat in a tight line. He'd only ever worn the same look when my dad had been ill. I jumped from my bed.

'Is something wrong, Grandad? Is it Tina? Is the baby okay?'

'Tina and the baby are fine,' he sighed. 'Sit back down. I need to tell you something.'

I frowned and lowered myself back onto my mattress. 'Okay…'

'The man in the accident today—Daniel. He died on the way to the hospital.'

'But… but he looked okay,' I said. 'He only had a couple of cuts. I put a plaster on his finger and everything.'

'It was all on the inside, John-Michael. Like when your dad was ill. We couldn't see what was going on inside him, and that was the same for young Daniel.'

Dad died before my tenth birthday due to complications caused by an undiagnosed stomach ulcer. I'd managed to get Tina to tell me a few years later. By the time the doctors had made a diagnosis, it had burst, and he died as a result of the infection that rapidly spread through his bloodstream, destroying his vital organs.

I scrunched up my face and flopped back onto my pillow. 'Oh, that's not fair, Grandad. I thought I'd helped him. I told him he would be alright!'

'Now, listen to me. Don't go blaming yourself for this,' he said. 'What happened couldn't have been prevented, and from what I hear from PC Williams, at least he had you to speak to before he lost consciousness. You should be proud he had someone with him in those moments.'

My eyes settled on Bruce Lee. 'Do you really think I helped him?'

'Yes, I know you did, son. Now, as I've said, don't you go thinking about this all night. It was an unfortunate accident. Okay?' Grandad said.

'Okay…'

But it wasn't okay at all. How could it be? I'd told Daniel he was going to be all right; he was no longer with us, and he'd never get to ride his scooter ever again.

'I'll see you in the morning, lad. Rest easy.'

After Grandad left, I got ready for bed and slipped under the sheets. I felt terrible, worse than I'd ever felt, even more so than when Nana B and Dad died, and that had been the worst event in my short life.

I tried to sleep, and when I did, the dreams that had plagued me earlier continued to haunt me. First, I dreamt of my dad, and I watched on helpless as he took his last breath and blood trickled from the side of his mouth. Then I saw Daniel again, with his glassy eyes staring up at me. I ran away, back towards the shops. In the windows, I could see the reflections of everyone I had ever followed behind me. Instead of me shadowing them, they were doing it to me.

'You can't do this!' I shouted. 'I'm the Mirror Man! I'm the Mirror Man!'

I ran faster and faster to get away, when The Suit stepped out from a doorway. He flashed a grin at me, and I looked him in the eyes. They were dark brown, almost black, and his teeth were too white. It was as though I was shrinking when he looked down into my face.

He whispered, 'No, I'm the Mirror Man.' Then he shrugged his shoulders, checked the cuffs on his shirt, turned, and walked away laughing.

I woke with a start, drenched in sweat, and with Grandad and Mum in my room. I could just make them out in the darkness, standing at the foot of my bed.

'You okay, sweetheart?' Mum said.

Sweetheart? She never calls me sweetheart.

'You were shouting,' added Grandad. 'What were you dreaming about?'

'Dad and Daniel,' I told them. I skipped the part about The Suit. I wasn't ready to share any details about him yet. At least not until I'd figured out who he was and what he wanted.

'You're safe now,' Mum whispered. 'I'm going to warm you some milk. It'll help you sleep better,' she said and disappeared.

'Ya mam is certainly better, don't you think?' Grandad asked when we could no longer hear her down the hall.

'I guess,' I said.

'I thought I'd told you not to worry about what you'd seen today,' he said.

I pushed my fists into my eyes, hoping to rub some sense back into me. 'I tried not to, but the more I tried not to think about it, the more I did.'

'Alright, don't worry. Is there anything you want to talk about?' he asked me.

'Not really,' I said. 'What time is it?'

'Just gone two,' he said.

'Is that all?'

He patted me on the shoulder. 'I'm off back to bed, if you're okay. Your mam will be back in a minute. Night, son.'

'Night, Grandad.'

As he left, Mum came back with the milk and left it on my bedside table. She even took the plate and mug from earlier.

'Night, John-Michael,' she said, closing the door.

'Night, Mum.'

I could get used to this, I thought as I sipped the warm milk. It had a slightly bitter taste to it, but I drank it all, anyway.

CHAPTER ELEVEN

THE STRANGE DREAMS HAD continued to taunt me all night long, except when I drifted back to sleep, I'd been chasing after The Suit as the townsfolk chased after me. We'd make it as far as the library, where he would skid to a halt, turn, and point his fingers at me as his toothy grin turned into a snarl. Mr Phillips's words would echo all around us like a voice from above: 'I know you'll do right by me, John-Michael.'

I woke up panting, and for a moment, I wasn't sure if I was still dreaming. I patted my bed several times before I was certain I was back in the land of the living. I wiped at my brow before I checked the clock. I was going to be late! This had never happened to me before. I rushed to get ready, almost tripping over as I pulled on my jeans and ran downstairs for a quick breakfast. Mum was singing while making tea and toast.

She looked over her shoulder as I came in. 'Morning, sleepyhead. I was just going to come and wake you up.'

I froze on the threshold. I didn't think I'd ever seen her in such a good mood.

She raised an eyebrow at me in one of the mirrors. 'You'll be late if you don't get a move on, so sit down and stop gawping.'

After a mug of tea and four rounds of buttery toast, I went to work via the shortcut through the orchard, keeping my head down. I had a lot of thinking to do, but I couldn't shake the vision of The Suit from my head. He'd been watching me as I looked in the safe. I knew I had to get a glimpse of what was in there.

The bell dinged above the door as I walked into Claude's Antiques. Claude didn't jump when I entered this time. Whatever had caused his anxiety had apparently faded away. He was busy cleaning a new vase on a small round table.

'Morning, Mr Phillips,' I said cheerfully, hoping he hadn't noticed I was five minutes late.

'Morning, John-Michael, how are you feeling today?' he asked.

'I'm good, thank you. How are you?'

He ignored my question. 'I hear you tried to help that man who got knocked off his scooter yesterday.'

I shrugged. 'I talked to him, that's all.'

'Well, still more than most would have done, anyhow.' He threw the duster down, then went to his desk and opened his diary to go over the day's appointments. 'Right, best get on. No time for chit-chatting yet,' he said without looking up.

'Yes, Mr Phillips,' I said.

He seemed to have recovered from his shock, but I still wanted to keep an eye on him. I knew he wouldn't tell me if I asked him outright; he was always careful with the questions he answered. If he didn't want you to know something, he ignored it. But I had eyes and ears; there were plenty of things I could do to find out what was going on, and it would take my mind off everything else happening in my life if I could focus solely on another matter.

I didn't have to wait long to catch a snippet of something useful. Towards dinner time, I heard Mr Phillips on the phone. He had his back to me, but I stayed hidden in the doorway, just in case.

'Yes, yes,' he said quickly. 'It's about the Durs Egg. I need to shift them sharpish…'

A Pause.

'I thought so, too, but I've been let down and no one else has got the money. You must know someone…'

'Of course, they're secure in the safe. No one's getting in there without a key.'

What on earth is a Durs Egg? I wondered. Whatever it was, I was sure it was the reason for Mr Phillips's bizarre behaviour—and maybe even The Suit's sudden arrival too.

And I had the perfect plan.

'Okay, thanks. Bye now.' I heard him place the handset down, then move in my direction. I quickly darted back to my workstation before he appeared in the doorway, looking over at me.

'Ready for dinner, lad?'

I nodded and tidied up my space before following him to the kitchen.

Claude and I always had our dinner together. We would reminisce about his wife while he made us sandwiches; it helped to know we had both lost someone special.

'What's for dinner today, Mr Phillips?' I asked as I sat at the small table.

'Corned beef and mustard. Our favourite,' he said as he buttered the bread.

'Great. You know, I was just thinking about Mrs Phillips. Remember when she made us that rhubarb crumble, and we had to pretend we liked it?' I laughed.

'I do, lad.' He laughed too. 'I think she secretly knew, though; she never did make it again.'

'I miss her,' I said as he placed my dinner in front of me before sitting with his own.

'Me too. Our breaks have never been the same since, have they?'

'No, they were definitely a lot longer when she was around, and we were never short of biscuits, either.'

He laughed again.

'Mr Phillips?' I said as I chomped on my sandwich.

'Yes, JC?'

I smiled. It was the first time he'd used JC since I'd asked him to—which then only made me feel bad for what I was about to do next.

'I was wondering if maybe you wanted me to service your pocket watch? I've never done it for you before, and I've worked here for eight years now,' I said.

Mr Phillips hummed and swallowed a mouthful of bread. 'You might be right about that, son. Fine, you can service it.' He placed his sandwich down, dusted his hands on his chest, then reached into his breast pocket. 'Be careful with it, won't you?' he said as he placed it on the table for me.

'Of course, I will,' I told him as I, too, dusted my hands, then reached for it. *What does he take me for? I take care of every watch I handle*.

'My grandfather gave it to me. It's very precious, do you understand?' he added.

'I'll take extra special care of it, Mr Phillips.'

'Before you take it in the back, help me with the flail first. I need it on top of the counter. It's being collected today.'

After I helped him move the flail, I got started on the next stage of my plan. I carefully opened the watch and used my tweezers to remove the brass key hidden inside. The key looked like it had been in the watch for a long time. It had to be a spare.

I wouldn't be able to put the next stage of my plan into action until someone came into the shop. I needed Mr Phillips to be distracted so I could open the safe.

I serviced the watch while I waited, and an hour later, the bell above the door rang. I looked through into the shop. Fersy and Clive were back to collect the flail.

'What's the verdict?' Clive asked.

'It's genuine, alright,' Mr Phillips said. 'Six hundred years old, give or take. Not worth a lot now, but worth hanging on to.'

Fersy squinted down at the thing. 'Know anyone who might be interested?'

I knew Mr Phillips would be deep in conversation for a while, so I snuck off to his office. I tiptoed through with the key gripped in my hand, then knelt in front of his old desk, making sure I didn't knock anything. I carefully turned the key, and the door opened. It creaked a bit, so I stopped and listened. I could still hear voices, so I carried on.

When the door was fully open, I peered inside. There were some tatty envelopes full of paperwork and plenty of small boxes, probably containing rings or bracelets. To the left-hand side was an odd brown box. I opened it up and inside found the key for the big safe.

I pulled out from under the desk with the new key in my hand, pushed the door closed, and crept to the back of the room where the bigger safe stood, too big to hide, but too heavy to steal. After listening one more time for their voices, I inserted the key and opened it.

Inside was large enough to hide in should you ever feel the need to, and at least half my height. Amongst the other items was the red case I'd seen a few days earlier. On top sat a receipt; it was a list of the items bought from the house clearance.

I scanned down the list. Towards the bottom was written, '*Two duelling pistols (Durs Egg).*' I put the receipt down, then carefully unfastened the clips on the red case and lifted the lid. Inside, tucked in a blue velvet compartment, sat a pair of guns.

I slammed the lid shut, fastened it securely, and closed the safe, locking it tight. I couldn't believe what I'd seen or what I'd been holding. I didn't like the thought of guns being in our town. What if someone got shot, or worse?

Mr Phillips was right to want to get rid of them—and quick.

Were those the items the family were trying to get back? Was The Suit working for them? Or did one have nothing to do with the other?

CHAPTER TWELVE

I WENT STRAIGHT HOME, avoiding people and the world around me to prevent myself from getting distracted. Instead of going into the house, I headed around the back to the cottage to see Fred. I used my secret knock, and he let me in.

'Well, if it isn't the town hero,' he greeted me and raised his arm. I'm sure it was to pat me on the back, but he quickly put it down again as I hesitated.

I frowned both at his words and his actions; he knew I didn't like to be touched. 'Huh? I'm not a hero.'

'Well, I suppose hero is stretching it a bit, but I've been told what you did for that Daniel fella.'

'I didn't really do anything.' I shrugged. 'I only spoke to him for a few minutes. Who told you? Mrs Kelly, again?'

'She did, actually, but I'd already heard all about it from your mam.'

'My mum told you?' I asked. 'I didn't think you two spoke much.'

'We've had our differences, yes. She'll speak to me now and again, though. Proud as punch she was when she told me. There's something different about your mam. Have you noticed?'

I had noticed. She appeared to have cut down her drinking, and she was being nicer, even going so far as to have full-blown conversations with me. It had been years since we'd really communicated like that.

I hummed. 'Mum has changed. She started being nicer after I witnessed the accident with Daniel, but maybe it's that mixed with the news of Tina's baby. And she's cut down on the wine.'

'Well, ain't that something?' he said, slapping his thigh as we sat down. 'And Tina's having a baby, is she? You kept that quiet, JC.'

'Sorry, must have slipped my mind with everything that's happened this week…' I said, rubbing my head.

'Had a rough week, have you, lad?'

I nodded.

He chuckled. 'Welcome to the real world.'

I had no idea what that was supposed to mean, and I didn't have time to ask.

'Fred, I came round to ask you something, if I can.'

He shuffled forward in his chair. 'You can ask me. Doesn't mean I can help or give you an answer.'

I frowned again. Fred never gave a straight answer of yes or no. 'Do you know what a Durs Egg is?'

'Hmm, sure do. He was a pistol and rifle maker. What do you want to know about him for?'

'Oh… I heard someone talking about it, and I wondered what it was, that's all.'

'Fair enough.'

'Is he dead now, then?' I asked.

'Oh yeah, long gone, JC. His guns are practically antiques now.'

'Great, you've been immensely helpful, Fred.'

'Oh, JC, I'm not going to pry into your business, but you remember, where there're guns, there's trouble,' he said.

'Okay, Fred,' I said cheerfully. I didn't want him to suspect anything might be wrong.

I left Fred's and walked slowly to the main house. It would seem Mr Phillips had got himself some antique pistols. They were probably worth a lot of money, too, otherwise he wouldn't have them locked up in the safe. The only puzzling part of the mystery was why he had to get rid of them quickly. Perhaps he felt the same as I did and didn't like having guns in the shop. I wasn't back at work until Tuesday now, and I was eager for the day to come around so I could find out more.

I went in through the kitchen and found Mum had started to prepare tea.

'Hi, love,' she said, spotting me in one of the many mirrors.

'Oh. Umm, hi, Mum,' I said. She'd caught me off guard with her bizarre niceness again. Most of the time she barely spoke when I walked past her.

'I'm making your favourite tonight. Sausages, mash, and onion gravy,' she said with a smile. I was beginning to enjoy seeing one on her face. It made her look younger, somehow. It was also refreshing to see her without a glass of wine in her hand.

'Are they best sausages?' I asked. 'I don't like it when they have gristle in.'

'I know that, son. I fetched 'em myself from the butchers. They're Cumberland, too, not the Lincolnshire ones.'

I didn't know whether to laugh or cry. Mum really had been taking notice of me all these years. Maybe I really should have given up all my peculiar ways; perhaps things would have been better for us all—Grandad included. He would love that we were getting along for the first time in years. I really would try to change my odd habits from now on. If Mum could continue to make an effort, then so could I. I liked having a proper mum taking care of me. I know Tina had tried her best, but it wasn't the same. Plus, I was about to dive deep into the adult world, and

I didn't have as much time for following people right now. The only person I wanted to follow was The Suit.

As I set the table for tea, I could feel it in my bones that things were getting better. We were going to improve together. I hoped one day soon I could look at all my family again—especially Mum, but that would take some time.

As we sat at the table, everyone talked and smiled like there had never been anything wrong with our little family. We had so much to look forward to with the arrival of Tina's baby and with Grandad rejuvenating the family business. Things couldn't look any rosier for us. He told me he had two more jobs booked in for Monday, and it would be a busy day for us. Mum even talked about getting a part-time job, which caused Grandad and me to exchange another surprised glance.

I only needed to find out what was going on in the little antique shop, then all my worries would be behind me.

Everything was going to be perfect.

CHAPTER THIRTEEN

I SPENT MY DAYS off keeping myself busy. I read the library books I'd borrowed as a distraction and because I wanted to prove to Tina and Pete the baby would be safe in my hands, should they ever need a babysitter. I also studied the journal entries I'd made. I hadn't realised how many people I'd followed until I flicked back through it. Since I'd started writing in it, I'd followed close to two hundred people, and that didn't include those I'd shadowed before I'd even thought of starting a journal.

The weird dreams continued to taunt me whenever I slept, though—except the endings were different now. Instead of The Suit turning and pointing his fingers at me, he now held the guns in his hands and aimed them at my chest.

On Sunday morning, I washed my bloody denim jacket. Mum even helped with my laundry. Thankfully, she didn't spot the blood; it would have been hard to explain what happened to her.

In the afternoon, Tina and Pete came round. She didn't eat much, said she got her morning sickness in the afternoon and struggled to keep anything down. Mum fussed over her and gave her tips on how to ease the queasiness in her stomach. When I was washing and tidying up the kitchen, Tina came to talk to me.

'It's like she's had a personality transplant.' She laughed. 'What have you been slipping in her tea?' she asked.

'Me? Nothing,' I frowned.

'I know, I know, JC. It's only a joke.'

'Okay,' I said, wiping down all the surfaces.

'It is nice to see. It's like we've got the old Mum back,' she said.

'You've always had the same mum, Tina. It's me who's had a different one to you.'

She stepped back and clutched her neck. 'JC...'

'What? Did you think I never noticed how different she was with me compared to you?'

'Well... I... never thought you looked at things in that way.'

'I didn't. Not back then, anyway. But things have become clearer; matters and words that have been said in the past are finally slotting into place, and I understand them now.'

'You do?'

'Yes, there's a whole list of things. But I've decided to forgive and forget and be better for our family's sake, and for the new baby.'

Tina's hand drifted from her neck, down to her stomach. She smiled fondly. 'Wow, John-Michael. I never thought I'd see the day. You're finally becoming a man.'

I slammed down the tray I was holding. 'That's the problem, Tina. I've been a man for a long time, but everyone around here still treats me like a child!'

'JC, that's not true at all!' she said.

'It most certainly is! I'm always kept in the dark or waved away when important matters are discussed. I'm tired of being treated this way.'

'JC... I... I don't know what to say.'

'What can you say?' I shrugged. 'You will never understand what it's like for me.'

Her pretty green eyes glinted in the reflection on the window as they filled with tears.

I turned to face her but kept my head down. 'I'm sorry, Tina, I didn't mean to upset you. Can I give you a hug?'

She laughed. 'Of course, you can, JC. Come here.'

I wrapped her in a giant bear hug. It warmed my heart to have prolonged contact with my sister. I never wanted to shy away from physical contact again.

⊷⊱⊱⊱⊱ ⊰⊰⊰⊰⊷

Tuesday morning came around, and new energy ran through me. I almost skipped to the shop, eager to find out more about the guns.

The bell above the door rang as I entered. Mr Phillips was whistling a merry tune as he walked around the shop with a dance in his step, writing in his ledger.

'Good morning, Mr Phillips,' I said, bemused at his sudden change in demeanour. Had he managed to get rid of the guns? 'You look happy today,' I said.

'And why shouldn't I be?' he said as he inspected an old desk. 'The sun is shining; the birds are singing. It's a good day to be alive,' he said.

'Well, I think it looks like rain…' I told him. I was certain it would rain at some point today; the sky resembled Grandad's stash of wire wool.

'We'll be quiet today, then. Perhaps we can have a treat at dinner. You can fetch some of them lemon curds from the bakery. You like them, don't you?' he said.

'No.' I laughed. 'I like jam tarts. You like the lemon curds.'

'Oh yeah, that's right.' He chuckled. 'Well, twelve o'clock on the dot, you take yourself off to the bakery, okay, JC?'

'Yes, Mr Phillips, I will.' Was he trying to get rid of me? I hesitated before heading to my workstation. 'Mr Phillips, why are you so happy today?' I asked, chewing on my lip. I was never normally this forward.

'Let's just say I think I've struck a deal for the rare antiques I told you about.' He tapped the side of his nose.

I sighed. 'Great!' I hoped that included the guns.

At twelve o'clock I went to the bakery. They were busy with the dinner time rush, and by the time I was served, the heavens had opened, as I'd predicted. I tucked the brown paper bag containing our treats under my jacket and ran back to the shop.

The open sign had been turned to closed.

I shook the rain from my hair as I entered and found Mr Phillips wasn't at the counter. I guessed he'd gone to make the sandwiches and put the kettle on, so I walked into the kitchen, expecting to find him standing there. The kettle had boiled and was still steaming. The bread had been sliced, ready to butter.

But Mr Phillips was missing.

I frowned. It was like Thursday morning was repeating itself. I returned to where I'd located him the last time he vanished, but paused just outside the backroom as I heard a voice I didn't recognise.

I edged closer to listen better, but they'd stopped talking. Taking a breath, I moved forward again to see who was in there with Mr Phillips. He hardly ever let customers into this area.

I stood at the entrance and clamped my hand to my mouth to silence my gasp, almost dropping our tarts on the floor. A man in a blue suit with chestnut hair was crouched on the floor in front of my workbench. He appeared to be searching for something, the way his arms were moving, and I could just see a pair of brown trousers and brown shoes poking out from behind him. I recognised the shoes; they belonged to Mr Phillips. He always tied his laces in a single bow. I also recognised the man bent over him. It was The Suit, and I shivered as my mind pieced everything together.

I froze as I watched him plunge an object into Mr Phillips's side. The action made me plunge forward too. Mr Phillips groaned out in agony. 'Stop! Please!'

Then I saw the shiny blood running towards The Suit's shoes.

I took a small step back, then another, until my foot tapped the edge of a box. Before I had time to react, The Suit whipped around, sprang up, and knocked me into the wall. The bag I'd been holding slipped from my grasp, scattering the floor with pastries. He pinned me in place and grabbed at my face as I tried to turn it the other way. He roughly pulled at my cheeks to turn my head in line with his. I tried to avert my gaze, but he only dug his fingers into my cheeks harder, so I shut my eyes tight.

'Look at me,' he said. His breath was hot on my face.

'No!' I shouted.

I searched for a record to play on my internal record player to escape from the horrid scene in front of me.

'Look at me, or I'll kill the old man,' he whispered in my ear.

My eyes sprung open at those words, and I met his gaze. His eyes were nearly black, like two lumps of coal, just like in my dreams. I wanted to yell and get away. I didn't like the look in his stare. If I could have found it in me, I would have removed them from their sockets so I wouldn't have to look into them ever again. The more I looked, the more I felt as though I would disappear into their blackness.

'Tell me where they are!' he said, spraying spittle all over my face. I tried to move my hand up to wipe it off, but he saw me shift and gripped my wrist, holding it tight against my side. 'Don't try anything stupid, boy. I can snap your neck in a second.' As he said this, he slid his hand down from my face to my neck.

'I… I…'

'Answer me!' he shouted.

'Are… W-what… where?' I stammered.

'The eggs, the eggs,' he said quickly, his head moving from left to right.

'I… I… don't know!'

The Suit hummed thoughtfully. 'I'm sure you do…'

I couldn't tell him. He'd hurt Mr Phillips, and they didn't belong to him. Plus, Mr Phillips didn't want anyone to get their hands on them. I could only presume he meant The Suit. It was down to me now to keep them safe; Mr Phillips was my friend. I had to honour his wish.

Mr Phillips groaned again.

'Is he going to be alright?' I asked.

'That depends on you,' The Suit snarled, looking over his shoulder. 'Now, tell me where they are,' he said. At that moment, he released my face and dragged me by the shoulder to the seat at my workbench. He shoved me down so roughly I almost toppled off.

'Stay there.'

I wiped my face with my sleeve and massaged my cheeks where he'd dug his fingers in. Thankfully, he hadn't drawn blood. I watched The Suit as he rubbed his smooth face and glanced frantically around the room. There wasn't one hint of stubble on his face, and his hair was perfect, not a strand out of place. Now I was beginning to think I'd given him the entirely wrong nickname. I wanted to escape from here into my head and play my records, but I had to focus. Now wasn't the time for my childhood escape methods.

I peered down at my feet and spotted Mr Phillips's pocket watch peeking out from under the chair. I could only look at my feet, otherwise, I would see Mr Phillips, and I didn't want to see him in the state I knew he was in.

'Can I tie my trainers?' I asked The Suit.

'What?' He turned to look at me but never bothered to examine my feet. 'What a flipping question. Do you understand the gravity of the situation you're in?' he asked.

'Not really,' I said. It was true I didn't have a clue. I was sure whatever I did or said would be wrong for the situation I'd found myself in.

'Well, blow me,' he said. 'Go on, tie your bloody shoes, you retard.'

I bent down and pretended to tie my laces, though they were, of course, already fastened. Instead, I scooped up the watch and deposited it in my pocket before he could see.

The Suit bent down to Mr Phillips again. 'Where are the eggs, Claude?' he asked.

Mr Phillips groaned louder, then spluttered.

'You'll tell me, Claude, or I'm going to hurt this retard assistant over here.' He looked back at me with his creepy smile, and suddenly tears were stinging my eyes. I hated being called that. The kids at school used to call me it before I stopped going. I wasn't a retard. I'd looked it up in the dictionary. There was no way a retard would be able to fix clocks like I can.

The Suit started checking Mr Phillips's pockets; I knew he wouldn't find anything, as he had been doing that when I first came in.

I had to get away from here. The nearest exit was the backdoor. I knew I could make it there before the front, but could I leave Mr Phillips here with this man? And if I left, what if he caught up with me? What would he do?

What about Tina, Pete, and the baby?

Grandad, Fred, and Mum?

It was all too much to handle.

My head pounded as though it would explode.

My breaths came thick and fast.

I saw my dad's and Daniel's glassy eyes.

Then—

CHAPTER FOURTEEN

WHEN I CAME TO, I was slumped on the floor, my knuckles were bloody and sore, and The Suit had vanished.

I scrambled over to Mr Phillips. The colour had drained from his face, his chest had stopped rising, and I'd seen that same glassy stare before. The shop had been ransacked, probably in The Suit's search for the safe keys and the guns.

I checked the safes. They were still locked.

I stood and turned in a slow circle, taking everything in.

Then I ran.

I ran out through the back door, and I ran through the alleys and back streets. I could hear heavy keys jostling in my jacket pocket. I pulled them out. They belonged to Mr Phillips. I shoved them back in my pocket as I carried on running, wondering how they had ended up in my possession.

I didn't stop running until I came to the community centre. I went and hid behind the bins at the back and sat on a dry patch in the corner.

I couldn't go home.

I couldn't go back to work.

Mr Phillips was dead, murdered by The Suit; the man who had announced in my dreams that *he* was the Mirror Man, not me.

What if they blamed it on me?

Why did my hands hurt? It felt as though I'd punched a wall over and over.

I brought my knees up to my chest and slowly rocked back and forth.

I had nowhere to go.

What if The Suit came back? For the guns, or for me?

Would he seek me out and kill me too?

When I thought about it, it wasn't really a question of would he, but *when* would he?

I shouldn't have left.

I should never have run.

I'd been wrong about myself. I wasn't a man at all. A man would never have run away. I was still a kid in a man-sized body.

And I was in big trouble now.

CHAPTER FIFTEEN

I HID IN THAT position until dark; rocking back and forth, jumping at every noise, and trying to make myself disappear from existence.

When I was younger, Mum said I sometimes had disruptive outbursts where I would sweep the ornaments off the mantlepiece or paint the neighbour's dog with green wall paint. I never remembered doing any of these things—especially to the dog. What had I been thinking? It was as though I blacked out from the world for a short period of time, and when I came back, Mum would be cleaning up the mess. I would get a clip round the ear after every incident, even though I couldn't recall what had happened. Luckily, I hadn't had one of those blackouts for an exceptionally long time—until today, that is.

I looked at my knuckles.

But what had I done?

I checked my watch; it showed ten to ten.

I'd missed my tea, and I was cold, tired, and dirty.

Would Grandad and Mum be looking for me? Would they even care I hadn't come home yet? Did they know about poor Mr Phillips? Would Mum think I'd killed him?

My mind threw dozens of questions at me, making me feel faint and dizzy like I had in the shop. I shook it away. I had to get up off the floor; my backside was numb, and I had to get inside. I wouldn't be safe here if The Suit came back.

The only place I could go was Fred's. I wouldn't tell him anything, not yet. Not until I knew how much trouble I was in.

I made my way to Fred's, taking all the paths where I wouldn't be seen by anyone still out at this hour. I had to be careful. The Suit could have been stalking me right now.

When I got closer to home, I checked for any police presence. There were no cars about, but all the lights were on. I went around the back, climbed over the fence, and walked up to Fred's cottage. I lightly tapped on the kitchen window, then the door. That was our secret knock.

He quickly opened the door and yanked me in by my arm.

'Hey!' I said, rubbing my arm instinctively. Oddly, the grab hadn't left me feeling weird, as it usually would. Maybe hugging Tina had helped with my aversion to people's touch.

'Where have you been?' he said through gritted teeth. 'And what's happened to your face and hands?'

'Nothing,' I said, tucking my hands under my armpits. I walked over to the only mirror in the living area and inspected my reflection. My cheeks were marked red where The Suit had squeezed my face.

'Doesn't look like nothing, JC. Tell me what's going on. I've had your grandad here twice saying you didn't come home from work, and now you turn up here, looking like you've been fighting with someone. Have you been home yet?'

'No…' I said, turning around to look at him. My gaze settled on his face, and I noticed he had a wonky eye. His brow furrowed.

'John-Michael,' he said. 'You're looking at me. You never look at me.'

'Oh. I am, aren't I?' I said, though I didn't take my eyes off him as I watched all the expressions his face contorted into. 'What's happening?'

He muttered something under his breath and rubbed at the back of his neck. 'You tell me. Seriously, what's happened to you, JC?'

I didn't know what had happened to me, but I was looking at someone in the eye for the first time since I was a toddler. It could have only been The Suit's doing; he must have done something to me when he made me look at him, as though he had snapped it out of me with those dark eyes of his. He had been able to look into my eyes without flinching, and he was far from unnerved by them. Though I was unnerved now. Would I be able to keep it up? I didn't think so now with the way Fred was looking at me as though I'd grown a second head.

'You're starting to scare me, JC. I'm off to fetch your grandad,' he said, reaching for the door handle.

I darted across the room and put myself between him and the door.

'No, you can't leave,' I growled. The noise my voice made startled me. I brought a hand to my stomach as I felt it churn. My body had reacted in a way my brain hadn't asked it to.

Fred held his palms up. 'John-Michael, calm down. Now, I don't know what's happened or what's going on, but I've never seen this side to you, and I'll tell you something, I'm not liking what I'm seeing.'

'Sit down, you're not going anywhere,' I said; my voice remained louder than I'd expected.

Fred sighed and backtracked to the sofa, where he sat with his elbows on his knees, watching me carefully.

I had a lot to process. I was doing what everyone wanted me to do. I had looked at someone without using a mirror. As the awareness of what I'd done sank into my brain, I realised it did feel strange and uncomfortable. And I knew my gaze could go either way now; I could sink back into the world of mirrors and reflections or fight against it.

Though looking at folk was the least of my problems now. What of my family? Would they believe me when I told them what happened? And what about the police? Would *they* believe me?

'Can't we talk about it?' Fred asked, his voice barely above a whisper.

'Not right now, Fred, I'm not ready, and I need time to think. Can you put the kettle on and rustle me up something to eat? I'm famished,' I said, hearing my stomach grumble again.

He looked at me like I'd asked him to cook me a three-course meal. 'Fine. But you're going to have to tell me something,' he said, getting out of his old, battered chair.

I waved him away and looked out the window at my house. All the lights had gone out except for the kitchen. Whether my grandad had stayed up or left it on for me, I didn't know.

'Couple of slices of toast, do you?' Fred asked from his kitchenette.

'Yep, thanks, Fred. I'm really sorry about this,' I said as he banged crockery and cutlery, taking his frustrations out on them.

'I'm going to need more than an apology,' he said, bringing back the toast and tea.

I hummed but didn't share anything.

'Do you want something to clean them?' he said, nodding towards my hands when I didn't speak.

'Oh.' I held my hands out in front of me to inspect them. I flexed them and winced. The knuckles were bruised, and the skin had been scraped off. They really did look as if I'd punched a wall. 'Yeah, I best get them cleaned up,' I said.

Fred fetched me a cloth and a bottle of TCP. I dabbed at my knuckles and removed the dried blood. I'd have scabs in the morning, and there would be no hiding it. I put the cloth in the sink and ate the toast. Fred sat at the table, drinking his own cup of tea, not taking his eyes off me as I moved around his home.

'Are you going to let on what's going on, or what?' he almost snapped at me.

'I can't tell you what happened yet. I need to work it out through my own mind first. I've got some decisions to make,' I said, sitting at the small round table.

'Well make 'em fast and get out of my home,' he said, slamming his cup down. 'I don't want myself embroiled in whatever you've done. I shan't tell your grandad I've seen you, but I want you out of here.'

'Fine. I thought we were friends, Fred,' I said, watching him intently. It was refreshing to see a face in the flesh. You couldn't always see everything in a mirror or reflections. Reflections were the worst, and some mirrors had distortions, diluting faces. In the flesh, I saw it all. Every pore, blemish, mole, and freckle. If I'd been able to see all these things before, I'd have a much better description of the people in my journal.

Fred didn't say a word, and I left, slamming the door behind me.

I paused on the threshold and looked at the ground. I noticed the laces on one of my trainers had come undone. I scratched my head; they should never have unfastened. I always tied them in a double bow like grandad told me to do. There was nothing worse than tripping over your laces or bending down all the time; it was a waste of good energy, he would say, and I needed all my energy right now. It had to be a sign: a sign of bad luck, I thought.

I needed somewhere to hide.

I couldn't return home and bring this to their door. What if The Suit found me there? There was no way I'd let him hurt my family. Instead, I headed to our abandoned car showroom. No one would ever think to look for me there.

I approached the drive and looked towards the entrance. Thick tall trees lined the drive to my left. I knew they were perfect to hide behind, and so I kept to the grass on the right-hand side to avoid my steps crunching on the gravel. That way, I would be able to hear anyone coming down our drive.

I headed away from home, into the dreaded night. I'd never been out this late. The dark couldn't be trusted with its shadows and eerie sounds. I preferred the light and its reflections.

I hesitated every few steps, listening to the sounds of the night. A light wind rustled the old branches, and one of them cracked. I flinched as it conjured recollections of Mum smashing my mirrors.

The wind blew louder and swished round my ears. A strange noise caught my attention; it was getting louder and louder, causing my stomach to roll. My eyes caught a flash of white. For a second, I thought it was a ghost, but it was only a discarded carrier bag stuck in a tree.

I released the breath I hadn't realised I'd been holding just as the bag escaped the branches and flew off into the night, then I carried on creeping towards the showroom. By the time I got there, my heart was practically beating out of my chest.

I located some old bits of cardboard, dusted them down to sit on and tucked myself into a dark corner. When my heart slowed down, I drifted into an uncomfortable sleep.

In my dreams, I chased The Suit after he killed Mr Phillips. I put my hand out to touch him, but he would get farther away from me every time I got near. He'd glance over his shoulder and laugh. He was the only thing I dreamt of all night long.

CHAPTER SIXTEEN

A CROW CAWED IN the distance, and I woke abruptly, yelling out Mr Phillips's name.

Light had started to creep through the gaps in the newspapers taped to the showroom's windows. As my eyes adjusted to where I'd slept, I roughly swept my hands through my hair, removing any debris that may have landed on me in the night. My shoulders hunched up as I cringed at the memories of yesterday and from having to sleep in an abandoned building.

Once the life and soul of our family, the building was now the only reminder of what had been. I shook the sad thoughts away.

I checked the time. It was still early, but I knew what I had to do next. I struggled to my feet after sleeping on the cold damp floor all night, then dusted off the rest of my body.

I had to do right by Mr Phillips like he had wanted me to. I had to get the guns. I couldn't let The Suit get them. He may have had them in my dreams, but I wasn't going to let him touch them or taunt me with them in reality. If I ever never needed power against The Suit, those were the tools to get it. With them in my possession, I'd be able to keep my family safe and be in control—like blackmail. Plus, I knew Mr Phillips wouldn't want them getting into the wrong hands; they'd be safer with me. This is what he meant when he said I'd figure it out.

I removed the keys and pocket watch from my jacket and hid them. There was an old-parts rack lined with fifty slanted pigeonhole boxes. I selected the sixth column down and the sixth box across and placed the items in carefully. I didn't want to end up losing them before I made my way back to Claude's Antiques.

I walked there slowly, hiding where I could in case Mr Phillips had been discovered and I had to conceal my presence. When I got to town, I pulled up the collar on my jacket in an attempt to conceal my face and dipped my hands into my pockets.

That's when I spotted him watching me from across the road. His face was swollen, bruised.

What happened to him? I wondered.

Two other men in black suits stood farther up the road from him. They were bigger, more menacing.

My stomach dropped. Had he brought his friends along to help get me?

This was bad.

The Suit moved to cross over, but the town bus passed by, blocking his path. I turned on my heel too quickly, losing my balance. At that moment, a cyclist who had decided to mount the pavement whizzed by. My flailing arms caught him, and we tumbled onto the pavement.

'What you playing at?!' the cyclist shouted at me, drawing the attention of PC Williams, who happened to be strolling by on the other side of the street.

I freed myself from the mess, shoving the cyclist's bike off me and into the road, and ran towards the shop. The Suit was nowhere to be seen, but I could hear PC Williams yelling after me.

I ran in through the unlocked front door. A sense of dread clung to me as the bell chimed, but I pushed it aside and dashed through to the backroom.

I hovered near Mr Phillips's body, though I didn't look. Instead, I turned and stared at the paper bag containing the remnants of our lemon curds and jam tarts. A pang of terrible guilt washed over me; I hadn't done a thing to help him.

The bell rang behind me. My time was up.

'John-Michael, why didn't you stop? Where've you been all night? Your mam and grandad have been worried—'

I remained still with my mouth shut as PC Williams arrived next to me.

'By 'eck...' He pushed past me and crouched, checking Mr Phillips for a pulse. I kept my gaze on the lemon curds, watching him from the corner of my eye. 'Did you just find him like this?' he asked, looking up at me.

'Yes... no... yes,' I stammered.

The constable stood quickly. 'Well, which is it?'

'Yes,' I said.

'Wait here,' he said.

I heard him use the phone, and I sat on the chair at my workbench.

'Did you do this?' he asked as he returned.

I shook my head. 'No, I never laid a finger on him. Honest!'

'Do you know who did?'

I bit my lip to hold back the tears. 'Yes.'

'Right, don't move. I'll be back in a minute.'

I didn't move an inch while I waited. I could hear sirens getting closer and closer until they were right out front. PC Williams returned.

'John-Michael, you'll have to come down to the station with me. Now, I'm not arresting you, but once we're there, you're most likely going to be their number one suspect. Do you understand what that means?'

'Yes, sir,' I whispered.

'Good. I don't think for one minute you did this, and I'll provide you with assistance the best I can, but you are likely in for a rough ride.' He went to take me by the arm, then apparently changed his mind. 'John-Michael, is what happened here the reason you never came home last night?' he asked.

'Yes. I was scared he'd follow me and get me too.'

'Alright, son. Come on.'

He took me out the front door, where a small crowd had started to gather, and put me in the back of the police car before going back inside with some other officers. I guessed The Suit had to be long gone now. I kept my head down as people walked up to the car to get a glimpse of the person in the backseat, and ten minutes later, PC Williams drove me to the station where another officer practically threw me in a cell.

Before the latch locked behind me, he whispered, 'You'll end up in Borstal. They'll love you in there.' I didn't know what he'd meant, but I didn't like the sound of it.

I inspected my surroundings. There was a fixed bench, and it stank of body odour, urine, and vomit with a layer of bleach lingering over the top of it all. I didn't like it in here, not one bit.

I banged on the door. 'When can I come out, please?'

No one answered.

I gently perched myself on the edge of the bench and folded my battered hands in my lap. I'd never been imprisoned before, and I imagined all the criminals who'd sat here in the past.

I hadn't killed Mr Phillips. But then again, I hadn't helped myself, either. I hadn't called the police when it happened, *and* I'd returned to the scene of the crime. Every finger in this town would point at me; the weird kid who couldn't look at anyone. I'd prove my innocence... somehow.

I didn't know how long I was in the cell for, but I managed to play two full albums on the record player in my head before I heard any sounds from outside the door.

Keys rattled, and the door swung open; PC Williams stood in the doorway. I glanced up as far as his mouth, which sat in a tight line, as though his lips had disappeared.

'Stand up, lad, you're going to be asked some questions now,' he said.

'About what?' I asked dropping my head.

'Two detectives are going to ask you about what happened to Mr Phillips.'

'But it wasn't me. I didn't do anything.'

'I know you didn't, lad. But it's not me you have to convince. You'll have to tell them everything you know. Do you understand?'

'Okay.'

'I'm going to be in the back of the room at your grandad's request. You can't have a parent or guardian with you, you're too old, but we've worked it out with the boss. Because of your… difficulties communicating sometimes.'

My eyebrows scrunched together. 'My communication is fine. I just need a minute sometimes.'

'Come on, son. We both know you aren't the same as everyone else. Best I'm in there with you.'

I chewed on my lip for a moment. Judging by the direction of his chin, PC Williams was looking at the clock on the wall, like it was too painful for him to look at me. I couldn't look at him, either. Whatever had happened to allow me to gaze at Fred's face had faded away.

'My grandad is here, you said. What about Mum?'

'Her too. They've both been speaking with the detectives. That's why you've been in here so long.'

My heart sank. They were bound to think it was me, since I hadn't come home last night. I had to tell the detectives about The Suit, but would they believe me?

Well, they would have to.

PC Williams took me through to a room that smelled like the ashtray on the table. He sat me down in a hard, blue chair and stood behind me with his arms folded. I eyed him in the mirrored glass in front of me. After a couple of minutes, two men came in dressed in brown suits. They both smoked. I lowered my head and focused on the scabs that had formed on my knuckles.

'This is Detectives Lightman and Green. They're going to ask you some questions, John-Michael,' said PC Williams.

The detectives sat down. One of them scraped the ashtray towards them, then blew his cigarette smoke in my direction.

'I'm Detective Green,' the man said. 'Do you smoke?'

I shook my head. I'd never smoked, but I could certainly do with a big glug of my grandad's best whiskey right now.

'We'd like to ask you a few questions,' said the other man, Detective Lightman.

Their two pairs of eyes stared at me intently, like I was a horrible murderer and should be sent to prison for the rest of my life. I kept my head tucked into my neck as a way of avoiding their burning stares.

'Do you know why you're here today?' asked Detective Green.

I nodded, then shook my head. I did know, but also, I didn't. None of this was my fault.

'Your boss Mr Phillips was found dead this morning by you and PC Williams. You better tell us everything you know about it, and don't leave anything out.' He raised his voice at the end.

I kept my eyes on my hands. 'What do you want to know?'

'Tell us what you did,' coaxed Detective Lightman.

I took a steady breath and focused to make sure my words came out in the correct order. 'I didn't do anything to him,' I told them. 'It *wasn't* me,' I reiterated.

'Do you know who did?' he asked.

'No. Yes, I mean—'

'Which is it?' interrupted Detective Green. 'It's a simple enough question, John.' He lit another cigarette and sucked it deeply.

'It's John-Michael,' I said.

'Fine, John-Michael, I'll ask again. Do you know who killed Mr Phillips?'

I nodded my head.

Detective Green slammed his hand on the table, making me jump. 'Who?!'

'I'm scared,' I said. 'He said he'd snap my neck.'

The other detective spoke now. 'We know you've had some umm... difficulties, but you're going to have to start telling us something, John-Michael.'

This time, I slammed my hand on the table. 'I'm not a retard!' I said.

'Hey now, easy, lad. No one's calling anyone any names here. We just want to know what happened to Mr Phillips. You're going to have to give us some answers soon, or we may as well have PC Williams put you back in holding until you can tell us.'

'No need for that, is there?' asked PC Williams from the back of the room. 'He said he didn't do it, and he's obviously scared. Give him a minute to tell you.'

'No.' I shook my head, closing my hands into fists. 'I don't want to go back in there. I want to go home.'

'Right. Well, if you want to go home, you're going to have to start sharing a bit of information. You better tell us the whole truth and not a *Jackanory*,' said Green.

'Okay, I know who did it. I know who hurt Mr Phillips,' I said, finally lifting my head for the first time in the interview. I looked over their heads at PC Williams's reflection. His eyes widened as he finally looked in my direction. The atmosphere in the room shifted as they all waited for my answer.

'The Suit did it,' I told them.

For a moment, there was only silence. Detective Green broke it: 'Who is The Suit?'

'I don't know, but that's the nickname I gave him. Mr Phillips asked me to go to the bakery to get some lemon curds and tarts for dinner, but when I got back to the shop, I found The Suit bent over Mr Phillips. Then he saw me and pinned me up against the wall and called me names. Said he'd snap my neck. Then I blacked out, and when I woke up, he'd gone, and my hands were bruised and sore. But I didn't touch Mr Phillips; he was my friend.'

The world began to blur as I was talking, but not because I was blacking out again. Hot tears burned my eyes and threatened to spill over.

The detectives mumbled between themselves.

'Do you know what he wanted?' Green asked.

'He was… looking for something,' I said.

'Looking for what?'

I shrugged and shook my head. I couldn't tell them about the guns. I got the distinct impression from Mr Phillips that he wouldn't want me to. I had to do right by him, and not telling them seemed right.

'Okay… Tell us more about this "Suit" character,' Green said.

I nodded. 'I first saw him last week when PC Williams took me home, then when Daniel died—'

'Daniel?' he interrupted.

'Young lad who got knocked off his scooter in that terrible accident last week,' PC Williams clarified from behind me.

'Oh right, yeah, carry on,' Green said.

'He was right there outside Claude's Antiques. He'd been outside watching for days. He was even there this morning. People must have seen him. He's been all over town.'

'Did you see anyone out of the ordinary this morning?' Green directed the question over my head to PC Williams.

'No one I didn't recognise,' the constable replied.

'You've got to find him. He doesn't belong here!' I said.

'What do you mean he doesn't belong here?'

'The way he dresses. He can't be a proper Yorkshire man,' I told them.

The three men chuckled, which startled me. How could they laugh at a time like this?

'Oh, aye. What's a proper Yorkshire man, then, when he's at home?'

I frowned at Green's jovial tone. 'Like you two or my grandad,' I said. 'He was different, not from round here. He was tanned with the same colour hair as me, but cut different and black eyes—not brown, black. He had a really nice suit on. Tailormade, blue like a shark. Three buttons down the front. The bottom one wasn't fastened. Small collar and narrow-fitted trousers. Really white teeth, like them on the adverts. I've written all about the times I've seen him in my journal, except for when he killed Mr Phillips. I haven't been home yet to write it down.'

I noticed Detective Green had started to write the description I was giving them down. I hoped they believed me.

'Can we see this journal?' he asked.

'Umm…' I wasn't keen on letting someone read my journal. They would see all the details of everyone I'd ever followed.

'It could really help us find this "Suit" fella. If we can read it for ourselves…' he prompted.

I bit my lip. 'Okay. But you're not to read anything else. Only his entry.'

He chuckled. 'Scout's honour,' he said, holding three fingers up. I wasn't sure if I believed him. 'PC Williams, get WPC Thompson to take his grandad back home to get the journal,' he told him.

'Righto,' he said and was just about to leave when I half-turned to stop him.

'Wait,' I said. 'He doesn't know where it is.'

I filled him in on where to find it, and we waited for them to return with the journal. During that time, the detectives made me repeat everything I'd told them over and over until WPC Thompson came back with the journal.

I unbound the book, located the page with The Suit's name at the top, handed it over, and waited while both detectives read it in turn.

'PC Williams, get WPC Thompson to copy this down exactly as John-Michael has written it, then bring it back,' said Detective Lightman.

The constable jumped from the back of the room and took the book. 'Back in a jiffy.'

'John-Michael, you said you wrote the first entry a week ago?' Detective Lightman asked as the door closed behind PC Williams.

'Yes, today a week ago.'

'And you'd never seen him before until then?'

'No, and I see everyone,' I told him.

'Yes, so I've noticed. That's a mighty heavy journal, John-Michael.'

PC Williams came back into the room with my journal and a slip of paper in his hands.

'That was quick. I hope she hasn't written it out in shorthand. I want it exactly as John-Michael has written it,' Lightman said to PC Williams.

'She's a fast writer, that girl. I checked it myself,' he replied, handing the paper to the detectives and my journal to me.

The detectives scrutinised the paper once more, then Lightman looked up at PC Williams, who had resumed his place behind me.

'What do you think, constable?' asked Lightman. 'You seen or heard about anyone new around town fitting this description?'

'Nope, but things have been hectic with the accident last week and extra shifts at the mine. I think the lad is telling the truth. I don't think he'd hurt anybody. What I can't fathom is why he didn't report it when it happened,' he said.

I bit down on my lip. What he was saying was right. I should have told them, and I wouldn't be in this mess.

'He's right, I wouldn't hurt anybody—especially Mr Phillips. He was my friend. Grandad's too. I was scared, so I ran and ran until I couldn't run anymore, then I hid. He said he was going to hurt me,' I stressed, then I remembered Mr Phillips's anxious behaviour. 'Mr Phillips was scared too. I found him hiding in a corner one day. He said something *bad* might happen to him.'

'Did he? Alright, son, we're going to make some enquiries. But you aren't off the hook yet, this is a serious murder enquiry. You best be praying your story checks out. Just 'cos PC Williams here believes you doesn't mean we do. Do you understand?'

I gulped. They had to believe me. 'Yes. Can I go home now?'

'Yes, with some conditions, but you'll be seeing us again, John-Michael. Keep your nose clean 'til then.'

'My nose is always clean,' I said.

I couldn't be sure who, but one of them snorted and then they both got up and left.

PC Williams came and sat in front of me, and I shuffled my chair so I could sit to the side.

'John-Michael, what a mess you've got yourself into,' he said, shaking his head. 'They could throw the book at you if your story doesn't check out.'

'I'm telling the truth!' I yelled with fists clenched on my thighs. 'The Suit is real. I would never hurt Mr Phillips. I love working in his shop.'

'Alright, I know you'd never hurt him. I'm going to ask around about this "Suit" fella. Someone must have seen him if he stands out as much as you say.'

'People had to have seen him. He's been hanging around for a week now.'

'Okay, come on. The desk sergeant needs to go through a few things with you. Then I'll take you to where your grandad and mam are waiting for you.'

Great. I was more scared of them than of the two detectives.

CHAPTER SEVENTEEN

MUM SLAPPED ME HARD across the face, and I stumbled back onto PC Williams's feet. He cleared his throat but didn't say anything.

'I knew you were a wrong'un, from the day you were born,' she said and stormed out.

'Grandad, it wasn't me!' I told him.

'I know that, lad, you'd never hurt anyone. It's just that me and your mam… we can't understand why you didn't fetch the police or tell us. We could've sorted out all this mess. What on earth were you thinking, John-Michael? I didn't bring you up that way.' he said, his shoulders sagging.

'I'm sorry…' My stance matched his.

'I bet you are, son. You're in deep crap now.'

I frowned. I knew it must be bad if Grandad swore. He hardly ever used foul language.

'Come on and get in the car. Tina and Pete should be waiting at home,' he said, gently touching me on the shoulder to guide me out.

'Why are Tina and Pete waiting, do they have more news to tell us?' I asked. I didn't think I could take on much more news.

'No, we're having a family meeting when we get back. We need to talk about this mess you've created.'

I sighed, 'Okay...,' and climbed into the back of the car.

No one spoke all the way home. At times it seemed like we weren't even breathing, as if no one dared make a sound, because if they did, then someone was sure to erupt. I was glad for the silence, though. It meant I could keep a careful eye on my surroundings as we drove home, checking for The Suit. He'd been watching me outside the shop, which meant he could be lurking anywhere, ready to pounce.

Once home, the three of us walked into the house to where Tina and Pete were waiting for us in the dining room. Tina was sat at the table with Pete stood behind her, dressed in his suit and with his hand on her shoulder. She looked like she'd been crying.

'Sit down,' Grandad told me. 'And you, Pete.'

I sat down, as did everybody else. I scanned their faces in the mirrors. They all looked grim and stern. It was several moments before anyone uttered a word.

'Did you do it?' asked Tina softly.

'Do what?' I asked.

'Oh, come on!' Mum shouted. 'Are you really that flipping stupid? Did you kill Mr Phillips?!'

'Mum!' Tina returned the shout, while Grandad banged his fist on the table.

'Of course, he bloody well didn't,' he said. 'This is our JC we're talking about. Not a bad bone in his body.'

I hung my head in shame. 'I didn't do it.'

'You what, John-Michael?' said Tina.

'I didn't hurt Mr Phillips. Do you really think I could do that?' I asked her.

At that, she seemed to sag with relief and gave a little sob. Pete put his arm around her. But she didn't answer my question. I expected this from Mum, but not her.

Grandad exhaled long and hard. 'See, what did I tell you? No grandson of mine is a cold-blooded murderer.'

Mum scoffed. 'Great, Stephen. Your words are going to stop everyone pointing the finger, are they?'

'Well, let's not think about that now. We've got other things to discuss.'

Mum buried her face in her palm. 'I'll never be able to show my face again...'

'Because it's all about you, isn't it, Mum?' Tina growled.

Mum looked up and rolled her eyes. 'God, I need a drink.'

At that, Tina promptly stood, almost knocking her chair over. 'Yeah, that's it, Mum. Drink yourself into oblivion! I thought you were cutting back?'

Pete reached out to calm her, but she didn't accept more than his arm around her waist.

Mum stood too. 'I was until *soft lad* over there turned into Peter Sutcliffe!' she snarled. 'I should have crushed more pills in your bloody warm milk.'

Tina's mouth hung open in a giant O, and I clenched my fists. Peter Sutcliffe? Pills? Is that why the milk tasted funny? She had slipped something into my drink.

Pete removed his arm from around my sister and clasped his hands in front of him on the table. 'Woah, Anna, that's a bit harsh,' he said. 'The lad said he didn't do—'

'What pills?' Tina interrupted. 'Have you been drugging our John-Michael?'

'It was just a couple to help him sleep after he witnessed the accident last week.'

'For God's sake, mother, you can't just be putting pills in his drink! What if the police find out?'

So, that's why I slept so well...

Mum exhaled loudly and left the table, heading to the kitchen.

Once the room was silent again, Grandad turned to me. 'John-Michael...'

'Yes,' I grunted.

'Why didn't you tell the police, or me, or Tina even? We could have helped you. We would never have thought you capable of doing something like this.'

I looked back down. 'I was scared. The man who hurt Mr Phillips said he would hurt me too. He wanted to snap my neck. He threatened Mr Phillips, said he would hurt me to get information out of him. But if he could do that to him, he could do it to me. I was scared he would follow me home and use you to get to me.'

Mum came back with a glass of whiskey. She even brought Grandad one too.

'Thanks, Anna.' He smiled grimly. Mum nodded.

I hoped she'd calmed down. I needed her to believe me. Well, not just her—all of them.

'And you've told the police all about this man, haven't you?' asked Pete.

'Yes, I told them everything. What he looked like, what he was wearing. Everything.'

'Good. See, Tina, Anna, Stephen?' Pete said. 'The lad was scared because his boss had been killed. Come on, can you blame him for running away and not saying anything? Put yourselves in his shoes for a moment. How would you react to seeing someone killed in cold blood?'

They all sighed and nodded.

'I'm sorry,' said Mum. 'I shouldn't have called you by that vile man's name.'

Everyone turned to look at her; now all our mouths hung open.

'What?' She shrugged.

The three of them muttered, 'Nothing,' but I stayed quiet, though inside I was smiling. It meant the world to have her back on my side. And what did it matter she'd put something in my milk? At least I'd slept better.

'Now that's all out of the way, we'll leave the police to find the man responsible. We've got important matters to discuss,' said Grandad.

'Was what happened not the reason you called us here, Grandad? We've both left work because of this,' said Tina, gently tapping her hands on the table.

'Yes and no. With the death of Mr Phillips, John-Michael inherits the antique shop and the flat above it,' he explained.

'I do?' I asked at the same time both Tina and mum said, 'You what?'

'How do you know this?' asked Tina.

'After his Mary died, he spoke to me about it. He had a will drawn up—both PC Williams and I witnessed it. It's all above board, legal and all that.'

'Blimey…,' said Pete.

'Did you know about this?' Mum addressed me.

'No, I knew nothing. Why would he leave it to me? What about his family?' I asked.

'They're all in Australia, and they ain't coming back to England anytime soon. He's never even met them, anyway, and he had no one else to leave it to. You don't think he'd let the government get their hands on it, do you? Have it turned into another one of them foreign muck takeaways?'

Pete shook his head, but no one else did. I think they were as shocked as me.

'Are you sure you didn't know?' Mum asked again, eyeing my reflection suspiciously.

'Mum, why do you keep asking him that? He said he didn't know. Quit it,' said Tina.

'I didn't know. No one tells me anything.' I folded my arms. 'You don't treat me like an adult.'

'I'm only asking since the police might think it's motive for… well, you know.'

'You've been watching too much television, Mum,' said Tina.

Mum rolled her eyes and snorted.

'John-Michael didn't know,' Grandad said. 'Mr Phillips, PC Williams, and I thought it best we didn't tell anybody until the time was right, which we thought would be way into the future.' He waved his hand away from him. 'But here we are now, and I admit it won't be easy when news of this comes out. As dramatic as it sounds, Anna is right. I think there'll be some finger-pointing and accusations until the perpetrator is caught, so best the shop stays shut for a few days. What does everyone say to that?'

Everyone nodded their agreement, except for me.

'Grandad, what about people picking up their watches? They'll be counting on me being there,' I said.

'Do you have numbers and names for these people?'

'Yes, I think so. Mr Phillips recorded everything in that ledger and Rolodex of his.'

'Good. Once the police say it's okay to go back in, you can get the ledger and ring them and explain what's happened.'

My gaze sank to where my hands twiddled on the table. 'You mean... I have to speak to them?'

'Yes, JC, this is your shop now. You're going to have to get used to it,' he said, his tone flat.

I gulped. I rarely spoke to the customers. Had no need to, really. Perhaps this would be the door I needed to walk through to become whole. If I could speak to random strangers in the shop, then maybe I could look at them too.

'I think I need a sip of that whiskey, Grandad.' I nodded towards his glass, which had a mouthful left. He slid it over to me, and I swallowed it in one, relishing the burn as it slid down my throat.

'I needed that,' I sighed.

Everyone laughed.

'Can I get something to eat now? I'm hungry,' I said.

'Sure, I'll make some cheese-and-tomato sandwiches. Does everyone want one?' Mum asked.

'Yes, thanks,' everyone replied in unison, including me.

Tina leant over to me once Mum had left. 'You've certainly won Mum over now. She'd have gone ballistic over this a week ago.'

'I know, it's certainly a massive change,' I told her. 'I like it.'

'She knows deep down you didn't hurt Mr Phillips. I think I would have run away too if I'd have been in your shoes. I've told you before she blames herself.'

'Why? Is it because of what she said about my eyes?' I asked her.

Tina shot up straight. 'You remember her saying that to you?'

'Yes, it echoes at the back of my mind.'

'You were so young. This whole time...' She trailed off. 'Ignore me,' she continued and then smiled. 'You have beautiful eyes, John-Michael. Don't let anyone tell you any different. Not even Mum.'

'I won't.'

'I think Mum wasn't well after she had you. She didn't mean any of those words. At least now she's trying to make up for it... in her own way.'

At that moment, Mum brought in the sandwiches and a pot of tea. We all sat there eating our dinner like nothing had happened. Though inside, I feared this was the calm before the storm, as I'd heard people say. Something was brewing in the air. I just didn't know what it was yet.

I needed the guns to be in my possession in case The Suit came back for me and my family. I had to protect them. When I got out of here, if they ever let me go, I would go back to the shop and get them.

CHAPTER EIGHTEEN

BEFORE I DISAPPEARED TO my room that night, I retrieved the keys and pocket watch from the showroom and hid them with my journal in its hiding place. I had loads to work through, so I did what I normally did when I had to think: I lay on my bed to talk to Bruce.

'What would you do, Bruce?' I asked. An easy question for Bruce to answer, not for me. He would have used his martial arts skills and kicked The Suit out of the shop. I didn't think he would have left Mr Phillips on the floor overnight, either.

Grandad said it would be a couple of days before we could go back to Claude's Antiques. Well, it wasn't Claude's anymore; it was mine now. Though it would forever be known as Claude's. There was no way I would be changing the name.

I was desperate to get back in the shop to check on the guns. I had to know they were safe, which I knew they were—I had all the keys—but that didn't stop me from worrying.

The Suit plagued my dreams that night, hunting down my family and demanding the guns or he would kill them all.

Pete returned the next day without Tina to speak to Grandad and me.

We sat around the dining room table and Mum fetched us cups of tea.

'Right, before I start, John-Michael, I want you to know you're to be part of all family discussions from now on, no matter what. Okay?'

'Yes, Pete.'

'Quite right,' agreed Grandad.

'Okay. I've instructed a solicitor from Edwards, Adam & Stars to represent our family, should we have any problems down the line.'

I smiled when Pete said, 'our family.' I was happy to have the whole family behind me, and I was certain that everything would go back to normal once Mr Phillips's killer was caught.

Grandad raised an eyebrow, and Pete raised his hand.

'Before you say anything Stephen, this is at no cost.'

'Good job. They sound very fancy, which also means very expensive,' said Grandad.

'You're right, they are.' Pete paused to clear his throat before continuing. 'A mate of mine from my university days works there. He owes me a favour. You don't need to worry.'

Grandad reached for the plate of custard creams Mum had left as he asked, 'What does he owe you a favour for?'

Pete waved his hand. 'It's really not worth sharing with you, but Tina knows.'

'Fair enough, say no more. Well, that's a stroke of luck. We'd never be able to afford a decent one unless we asked JC here to sell some of the items in the shop sharpish.'

I gulped at the thought. Everything in Claude's Antiques now belonged to me. But I was glad Pete had been able to help us out, though I hoped we wouldn't need to use the solicitor's services.

'Oh, before I leave, John-Michael, I'm going to take you to open a bank account next week; you'll be needing it to pay expenses, bills, and rates.'

'Huh?' He was saying things I'd never heard of before.

Grandad slammed his hand down on the table. 'No, no. Absolutely not. He is not having a bank account. You can't trust banks. That's how the government keeps tabs on you, by checking what you spend your hard-earned cash on.'

Pete started laughing. 'Come on, Stephen, do you trust me?'

'Well, of course I do. I wouldn't have let you marry Tina if I didn't.'

I watched Pete frown at that. 'Then this is what JC needs to do. What do you say?' he said, turning his attention to me.

'Okay.' I said, much to Grandad's disapproval.

Pete left us with a few business cards with the solicitor's information, telling me to put one in my wallet, should I ever need it.

As we saw Pete out the door, PC Williams was walking up the drive. He tipped his head to Pete as they passed one another, and Grandad invited him to sit at the dining room table, rather than the kitchen one. He still had that weird look of amazement on his face as he sat down, surrounded by my mirrors. Mum cleared away the used cups but didn't bring any fresh ones.

'Stephen, John-Michael, I've come to give you a bit of an update, see'n as we're mates and all that,' he said.

'I really appreciate you being with him down at the station. You know he didn't do this,' Grandad started saying.

PC Williams held his hand up. 'I know that, mate, but I'm still the police, and I'm treading a fine line getting involved, what with how close we are. Anyway, it's not me you need to convince, it's the detectives that need winning over—plus the rest of the townsfolk. You know more than anything how they can be. People always judge first and ask questions later. They've already got him marked as guilty and are poised to throw away the key.'

'I suspected as much,' Grandad sighed. 'We're best off staying out of people's way until things calm down a bit, aye, lad,' he said to me.

'Okay, Grandad.' I chewed on my lip. Would the people in town chase after me like they had in my dream?

'Anyway, for now, the detectives are treating this as a robbery gone wrong with this "Suit" fella as the prime suspect. However, John-Michael is still a person of interest, especially as he ran away from the scene.'

I looked down. I was mighty sorry about that.

'I guess that's good for now,' said Grandad.

'Well, I don't know about that. You see, I've been asking around about this "Suit" man, and not one person I've spoken to recalls seeing him about town. Not the shop owners or other officers. Unless I can find someone who can validate John-Michael's story, then we've only got his word for it.'

I slammed my hand on the table. 'He is real, Grandad, he is! You need to find him, officer. Find out who he is!'

'I know, John-Michael. You just leave that to us, young man. Now, they'll have more questions for him at some point. They'll probably want to ask him about what happened again. Sometimes memories come back, and he hasn't signed a witness statement yet, either.'

Grandad sighed. 'Fair enough, we'll deal with that when it comes. Anything else?'

'Yes. The crime scene investigators have finished. You might want to get down the shop and check on things, and I'd change the locks if I were you.'

Grandad's eyebrow raised. 'Have they? That was quick.'

'I know. Far quicker than I expected for a murder. I just hope they've not taken any shortcuts in this. I'd hate to see young John-Michael get fingered for it over police incompetence,' he said, putting a hand over his badge.

Grandad shook his head. 'We have to hope it doesn't come to that.'

'I know I'm police and shouldn't talk ill of my colleagues in blue, but I've seen it before when mistakes have been made.

Anyway, enough of that talk. Have you told him about the shop?' he asked.

'Yeah, we told him about it yesterday.'

He nodded at me. 'You've got some big shoes to fill, lad,' he said.

'I haven't. Mr Phillips was a seven. I'm a nine.'

'I didn't mean that, son, it's only a saying. What it means is, you've got to do a good job in your new position as owner.'

I nodded back.

'Do your colleagues know he owns the shop now?' Grandad asked.

'Not yet, but they're sure to find out soon enough. I best be off now. Got a stack of paperwork to finish. I'll see myself out,' he said, putting on his helmet. 'I'll keep you updated where I can, Stephen.'

'Thanks, pal, I really do appreciate you sticking your neck on the line for John-Michael.'

He nodded and left.

Grandad stood from the table. 'Right, come on then, son.'

I didn't follow. 'Why, where are we going?'

'You heard the officer. Them locks need changing. No time like the present. I'm off to dig out some locks from the kitchen drawer, and you can go fetch my green toolbox from the garage. The green one, not the blue one.'

I rolled my eyes. 'Yes, I heard you. The green one.'

'Meet me at the car in five minutes,' he said. 'Oh, and bring any keys you've got. May as well retrieve the copy of the deeds and the will from the safe. The originals are filed with Mr Phillips's solicitor.'

'Why do you need them?' I asked.

'To make sure we fulfil his wishes.' The words caught in his throat, and he quickly walked away.

I went upstairs to get my keys, then went to get the toolbox.

'Where you off to?' Mum shouted behind me as I made my way to the garage. I turned to see her putting rubbish in the bin.

'To get Grandad's toolbox. We've got to change the locks at the shop.' I told her.

'Right, I'm coming too. Don't leave without me,' she said before hurrying back inside.

I arrived at the car as Grandad and Mum exited the house. Mum's arms were piled high with cleaning products. We loaded up the boot and set off.

Fifteen minutes later, we entered through the back door of Claude's Antiques. Grandad said it would be better to park behind the shop, so as to not raise people's suspicions. He went in first, advising it would be best not to look in where Mr Phillips died until we could clean up in there.

'I can't believe all this is yours,' said Mum as she took it all in. She'd never been in the shop before.

'I know, but it's a shame it had to happen this way,' I said.

She reached up and ruffled my hair. 'I'm going to clean up where it happened. You two can stay here.'

'Are you sure? Might be a bit... gruesome,' said Grandad.

'I'm sure,' she said, rolling up her sleeves and pulling on a pair of marigolds. 'Will be no good for your knees getting down on the floor, and I don't want John-Michael to have to see it.'

'Fair enough. You crack on, and we'll get the paperwork from the safe and change the locks,' he said, leading me to Mr Phillips's office.

'Hang on, Grandad, the key to the small safe is in the back of his pocket watch. I need my tools,' I said, pointing to the room where Mr Phillips was killed.

'Oh.' Grandad scratched his chin. 'Wait here. I'll get the tools you need.'

'But...'

'But nothing. I know what tools you'll be wanting. I've been repairing watches for longer than you've been alive, lad. Off you go. Wait for me in the office,' he said, waving me off.

I skulked off to the office and sat at the desk, my desk, to wait for the tools. I checked the safes while I waited. Both appeared secure and untampered with, but with Grandad and Mum around, it wasn't wise to check on the guns yet. It was a few minutes before Grandad returned, and I wondered what was taking him so long. When he appeared in the doorway, he appeared upset.

'Are you alright?' I asked him.

He sat opposite me and placed the tools on the desk. 'Yeah. It's a bit hard to come to terms with, is all. I half expect him to walk through the door and ask us what the hell we're doing back here. Do you know what I mean?'

I hummed. 'I think so. I keep waiting for him to shout to put the kettle on.'

'It'll get easier with time, son. Now, while your mam is out of earshot, why don't you tell me how you knew his key was in the pocket watch and how you came to be in possession of it?'

'Did I tell you about the day I found Mr Phillips hiding in the corner behind an old tea chest?'

He shook his head. 'No. When was this, and did you tell the police about it?'

'It was the morning of Daniel's accident, and yes, I told them. I've told them everything.'

Except I hadn't told them everything. I'd kept the details about the guns to myself. I needed the guns. No one else could protect my family except me.

'I came into work, and I couldn't find Mr Phillips anywhere. Eventually, I found him hiding behind an old tea chest. He looked scared, things were out of place, and he told me if anything should ever happen to him, I'd find the key to his small safe in the back of his pocket watch.'

I watched as Grandad sat back in his chair, lowered his head, and rubbed his temples.

'It's looking like old Mr Phillips knew something was going to happen, it would seem,' he finally said.

'I asked what he thought was going to happen to him, but he wouldn't tell me. You know how he was with questions.'

He laughed. 'Aye, if he didn't like a question, he'd ignore it. And the pocket watch, how come you had that?'

'The day it happened…' I paused and bit my lip. 'I found it on the floor. He must have dropped it. I pretended to tie my laces, and I slipped it in my pocket.'

'Do the police know you have it?'

I shook my head.

'Right, best keep that part between us.'

I got to work on the watch to retrieve the key, then pulled out all the envelopes from the safe and handed them to Grandad. He said he and Pete would go over them, and if there was anything in them I needed to know, they would tell me.

After we finished in the office Grandad went to the back door and got to changing the locks. I watched him as he worked. He said I would need to learn to do these things now I was the owner of the shop and flat. Once he was done with the back door, he handed me the tools and we walked to the front of the shop.

I went out the door, intending to pull down the shutters and hurry back in, but I paused as I exited and looked at the shop windows across the road. I already missed being able to walk past them without a care in the world. I'd have to curb my habits even more so now I was in charge of a whole shop.

I turned and reached up for the shutters. Behind me, loud footsteps echoed down the thin alleyway between the hardware shop and the greengrocers.

I paused with the shutter a third of the way down and used the reflections on the antique shop window to see who was about to exit. In the shadows, I saw a suit. He'd returned to get me.

'Grandad,' I whispered. The shaking of my hands caused the shutters to gently rattle. 'Grandad. Psst!'

'What's up, lad?' he said, poking his head out the door.

I looked back to the mirror image of the alley as a man emerged. It wasn't The Suit, just a man all dishevelled with his shirt untucked and his tie flipped over his shoulder.

'Nothing, Grandad. I'll be in, in a moment.'

I took one final glance around the street before pulling the shutters the rest of the way down.

Grandad instructed me on how to fit the new lock on the front door. He told me I could keep his toolbox in the shop; he'd even put a few extra locks in, just in case. I added the new keys to the set, then we switched off the lights and headed home.

CHAPTER NINETEEN

THAT NIGHT, AFTER RETURNING from Claude's Antiques, dreams disturbed the little amount of sleep I managed to snatch.

I was returning to the shop from the bakery, but as I walked, it felt as though my feet were weighed down with cement. The bell above the door continued to ring and ring, even though the door had closed firmly behind me.

Time seemed to leap forward, and before I knew it, I was stood watching The Suit plunge a sharp object into Mr Phillips's side. I almost fell forward, but my weighted feet steadied my swaying body.

'Mr Phillips!' I yelled.

The Suit turned and sneered at me.

'Do right by me, John-Michael,' Mr Phillips spluttered.

'I will, Mr Phillips.'

Time skipped ahead again, and I was pinned against the wall. Our baked treats splattered all over the floor.

The Suit leaned into me and whispered, 'I'm going to kill the old man.'

My head pounded as though it would explode.

My breaths came thick and fast.

I launched myself from the chair I was now seated on and attacked The Suit.

My fists pounded into his face until I collapsed in a heap on the floor.

CHAPTER TWENTY

A COUPLE OF DAYS passed, and we mostly stayed at home to stay out of people's ways and avoid the gossip. Grandad even took Mum grocery shopping in Doncaster where no one knew us; she didn't want the funny looks in the shops.

Grandad didn't have any work on, as the people he'd booked in for jobs either didn't show up or called to cancel. I'd managed to call the people whose watches I had and arranged for them to come in the following Monday morning. I was proud of myself for speaking to them without my words coming out all jumbled.

I constantly checked all the doors and windows at home after everyone had gone to bed to make sure we were safe. Also, I slept less and less as I worried about The Suit coming to find me, and the dreams didn't help matters.

As the dreams continued, I realised they were not dreams at all, but memories.

When I first dreamt about punching The Suit, I thought I was manifesting what I wished I had done, but when I pieced together all the fragments of the missing moments from when I blacked out, it was evident I hadn't really blacked out. I was still functioning in the world. It had been like the incidents when I was younger, though I couldn't remember those.

The dreams revealed I had beaten up The Suit. I'd gone nuts, crazy, mad, whatever you want to call it. It had been the reason why I'd come around with my knuckles bruised and bloody. I'd gone wild, launching myself at him, punching him over and over again. He hadn't seen it coming. It was why the place looked like it had been ransacked. His face had been a bloody purple mess. I figured he'd left sometime before I came to, though how no one had seen him leave was a mystery. He would have looked a state, and one of his eyes had been half shut, just like when I saw him the next day outside Claude's Antiques.

Monday morning arrived, and I staggered downstairs after another restless night. I had to open up the shop so the people I'd called up could collect their watches.

'Morning, son,' Mum said from the kitchen table.

'Hey, Mum,' I said, ending on a yawn.

'Aren't you sleeping?' she asked.

I looked in the mirror. Her face was etched with concern.

'No. Bad dreams.'

She hummed. 'If you ever want some of my pills, let me know. And I'm sorry I gave you them before without your knowledge; that was wrong of me.'

'It's okay, thanks, Mum,' I said, forcing a smile onto my face.

'Tea and toast?' she asked.

'Yes, please.'

I sat down, and Mum busied herself preparing my breakfast.

'So, it's the first day opening up on your own...' she started, her voice light.

I nodded, my jaw tight. I couldn't decide whether the prospect made me excited, sad, or scared. There was so much to think about; the responsibility, the customers, the watches, Mr Phillips's memory, The Suit coming back for me...

When I didn't reply, Mum continued, 'Say, I was thinking, why don't I come work in the shop with you?'

I stared at the back of her head in the mirror. 'You really want to help me?' I asked.

'Sure, I do,' she said, turning around. 'I can be up front with the customers, and you can carry on repairing the watches.'

'But you don't know anything about antiques,' I said in an attempt to put her off.

'Do you?' she said, returning with my tea and toast.

'Not much.'

'Then we'll learn together, won't we?'

I relented. I couldn't say no, especially since we were starting to bond and rebuild our relationship.

'Okay, Mum. I'd really like it if you helped me.'

'Great, get that down ya. You'll need a good breakfast to start each day. You'll be working six days a week now, John-Michael.'

I'd only worked three days a week until now. But I didn't mind. It meant I could provide for the family—as long as the customers returned.

Mum and I jumped in the car after breakfast and went to open up. She chatted to me excitedly all the way there. I smiled at her enthusiasm, but deep down I was worried that The Suit would return. I would not only have to protect myself but Mum too.

Mum took the route to the front of the shop.

'Mum, don't you think we should park around the back?'

'Oh… yeah, maybe.' Her fingers tapped the steering wheel nervously. 'I'm a little excited; I wasn't thinking. I'll turn round at the bottom of the street.'

'Okay—'

'What the—' I watched in the reflection on the passenger-side window as she sat right up against the wheel. 'Is that—?'

I followed the direction she seemed to be looking. Claude's Antiques had just come into view down the street, and there was something on the shutters.

She muttered something I couldn't hear and brought the car to a halt opposite Claude's Antiques. Someone had spray-painted 'Murderer' in black across the front.

'Should we go home?' I asked.

'What on earth for? From now, we will hold our heads up high and be brave. Why should we skulk off like wounded animals?'

'What are we going to do, then?'

The driver of a car behind us pipped its horn, and she drove off.

'I'm going to turn this car around, and we're going to open the shop, alright?'

'Okay, Mum.'

After parking round the back, Mum didn't bat an eyelid as she got to work on scrubbing the paint from the shutters. When she finished, she came in and made us both cups of tea as though nothing had happened.

'Thanks for taking care of that, Mum,' I said as she handed me my tea.

'Don't mention it, son. We've got this. I'll never let anyone say a bad word to your face, and if they spray it on the shop… Well, I'll clean it right off.'

Throughout the morning, customers arrived to collect their watches and offer their condolences for Mr Phillips's death with promises to return, which I was thankful for.

By the afternoon, Mum and I were sat behind the counter on two wooden stools we'd dug out from the storage room, having cups of tea. I had no new watches to repair, and I thought I'd keep her company. We were chatting about Tina's baby when two figures appeared behind the glass of the shopfront.

The two detectives, Lightman and Green, came in wearing identical brown suits I'd seen them in the first time we met, but this time I could see their faces properly in the various mirrors around the shop.

Detective Lightman was a head taller than Detective Green. He had thick, curly brown hair and a weird goatee. It looked like his moustache had fallen off and landed underneath his lips. Detective Green was all blond hair and blue eyes. He wouldn't have looked out of place on the television. They walked in slowly, pretending to browse items and running their fingers over the inventory. I didn't know what they expected to find; everything had been cleaned by me after the crime scene team had been in. There wasn't a speck of dirt on anything.

'Afternoon,' Mum said. 'Can we help you?'

'Yes, we'd like to take another look around,' said Detective Green. 'Perhaps in Mr Phillips's flat and check out the contents of his safes. It turns out the crime scene team were unable to find the keys and get access. We thought young John-Michael might know where the keys are and let us in.'

I frowned. I didn't want them looking in the safes or moseying around Mr Phillips's flat when we hadn't even been in there yet.

'Don't you need some kind of permission for that?' she said, eyeing the two men suspiciously. 'What's it called? Umm…' She started drumming her fingers on the counter.

'A warrant?' Detective Lightman offered.

'That's it, don't you need a warrant to snoop around?'

'Mrs Chester, we aren't snooping. This is a murder investigation, if you'd forgotten.'

'How could I? It's me who got down on my hands and knees and scrubbed the floors where Mr Phillips died,' she said, crossing her arms.

'We were hoping you would open the safes, John-Michael. If you have the keys, that is?' asked Detective Green, ignoring Mum's comment.

'I'm not so sure I should let you do that without permission,' I mumbled, 'like my mum said.'

'That's your right, John-Michael, see'n as you're the owner, so we've been told, but it would be much easier if you let us look now. You are the only witness to this, and we could really use your help,' he said.

Mum stepped in. 'Don't you try to manipulate my son. If he says no, that's it. Come back when you have a warrant—then you can search to your heart's content.'

'Alright, Mrs Chester,' said Lightman. 'Oh, and John-Michael, we want you down the station tomorrow afternoon to make your written statement and go over a few things, see'n as we've been unable to locate this "Suit" fella.'

'Don't forget your warrant next time,' Mum huffed as they left.

'Thanks, Mum.' I smiled at her.

'No thanks necessary; I'm your mam, and it's about time I stuck my neck out for you,' she said, then pulled her lips to the side. 'Where's the number for that fancy solicitor Pete gave you? He'll know what to do. We can't have them bizzies snooping around like they own the place. You've told them who did it. They should be out looking for him, not bothering us.'

'It's in my wallet,' I said, standing up and pulling my wallet from my back pocket.

She examined the card when I handed it to her and went to the phone tucked in the corner behind the counter.

'Umm, hello, yes. Can I speak to David Mercier, please?'

'Yes, it's Mrs Chester, Pete Newman's mother-in-law...'

She pulled her head from the handset and turned her attention to me. 'They've put me on hold; there's a weird beeping sound. Do you want to listen in?'

'No, you do it.'

She started tapping her foot, then suddenly stood up straight again.

'Hello, Mr Mercier. Yes, Pete said you'd be able to help us if we had any problems.'

'Well, two detectives came round. They want to look in the safes and the flat upstairs and then they want our John-Michael in for a statement.'

'No, we didn't let them, they didn't have a warrant...'

'Good, I thought I was saying the right thing. What should we do now?' Mum asked as she twirled the telephone cord around her finger.

'You will?' Her eyebrows raised. 'Okay, I will. Thank you, Mr Mercier.'

'Oh, I'll certainly do that. Thanks again. Goodbye.' She placed the phone down, then puffed her cheeks out and slumped against the counter.

'What did he say mum?' I asked.

'He's going to take care of it.'

'Is that it? It was an awfully long conversation, Mum.'

She laughed. 'It wasn't that long, JC.'

I cocked my head at her. She never called me JC.

'What?' she said, mirroring my cocked head.

'You never call me JC,' I said.

'Oh.' She looked up as though exploring her memories to see if I was right. She didn't need to search. I know she never used JC.

'It's okay, Mum. I know we've had our, umm... differences, but we're moving past that now, don't you think so?'

'I do, John-Michael, I really do. Everything you've done and become is all because of me; the lack of attention and the nasty comments about your eyes are all things a parent should never do or say, and I take full responsibility for that.' Her voice cracked, but she continued. 'I'm going to do my absolute best to make it up to you. I've been a terrible mother, but I'm going to help you, be there for you, and maybe help you to look at us like you used to.' She pulled out a hanky and wiped her nose. 'Okay enough of the soppy stuff, what was I saying?'

I ran over and hugged her tight, almost knocking her over. I can't remember the last time I'd had physical contact from her besides a clip around the head.

'Oh, John-Michael,' she said, hugging me back. 'I've missed so much.'

'So have I mum,' I said into her hair. I was much taller than she was.

I liked hugging her just as much as I'd enjoyed the prolonged one with Tina. Mum said she'd missed so much, but then so had I. Though I didn't like the fact it had taken the deaths of two people to bring us back together as proper mother and son.

'Right, no time for this now,' she said, removing my arms from her waist. 'I need to tell you what that solicitor said before I forget. He said he'll find out what evidence they have to substantiate a warrant. They must think something is here for them to get the warrant, or something to that effect. He also said he knows plenty of magistrates and putting a stop to the warrant won't be an issue. If they come back, we're to tell them to ring him. He's our solicitor now, and all questions are to go through him. That was about the gist of it.'

'Can he really do all that?' I asked.

She shrugged. 'He says so.'

'What about the statement?'

'Oh, yes he'll meet us there tomorrow at two.'

We decided to shut up early and left through the back door. We weren't ready to be seen out in public yet, seeing as people wouldn't believe I hadn't done it and The Suit hadn't been caught. Mum said she was sure things would calm down in a week or two. I wasn't convinced by her optimism.

CHAPTER TWENTY-ONE

THE NEXT AFTERNOON, IN a blustery headwind, I walked with Mum to the police station. She said the fresh air would do us good, but it only made my face sting and eyes water. Mr Mercier met us there, though, and we waited in the same room I was interviewed in almost two weeks earlier. Mum wasn't allowed in and had to wait outside for us to finish.

'We have some time before the detectives come in, so I want to take this opportunity to properly introduce myself and update you on a couple of things,' he said. He didn't look at me I guessed Pete had told him not to. Instead, he focused on the paperwork he had in front of him. 'I work for Edwards, Adam & Stars. Pete has probably told you this. Anyway, I'm a barrister, do you know what that means?' he asked, shuffling his papers.

'No, I don't, sir.'

'It means I'm usually in the courtroom, not seeing clients in this setting. So don't be surprised if the detectives are stunned to see me.'

'Okay, sir.'

'Moving on, the detectives are trying to obtain a warrant so they can do a thorough search of Claude's Antiques, including the safes and the flat above. Now, I don't want you to worry. I can keep them tied up for weeks in paperwork to prevent that from happening. Plus, I know every local magistrate for miles, and I've a sleeve full of favours that can put a stop to anything. Are you with me?' he asked.

I nodded, but I was a little confused with all the talk of favours. I didn't know what Pete had done for Mr Mercier, but it must have been pretty big for him to go to these lengths for me. Is this what adult life was really like, owing favours to one another?

Regardless of if they got the warrant, they wouldn't find the guns. I was going to remove them after we were done here and take them home for safekeeping. I'd been trying to think of a way to get them home without anyone seeing, and this was the perfect opportunity.

'Great. Pete has filled me in on the majority of what happened, and I've got snippets from the police. Is there anything you'd like to share with me?' he asked.

I hummed. I'd been holding back from telling Mum, Grandad, Tina, and Pete much about what I was thinking and feeling. I didn't want to worry them or tell them more than they needed to know, for their own safety. And in truth, I felt like my head was going to explode sometimes.

'It will be just between us,' Mr Mercier added.

I bit my lip. 'The Suit. The man who killed Mr Phillips. He's haunting my thoughts and dreams,' I told him hesitantly, though I was relieved to finally say it out loud.

'I see.' He cleared his throat. 'And this is the man the police have been unable to track down?'

I nodded.

'Okay, John-Michael. Don't you worry now.'

We sat in silence until detectives Lightman and Green walked in. They turned to each other as they entered. I imagined they were giving each other bemused glances, just as Mr Mercier said they would.

'Mr Mercier. Nice to see you again,' said Detective Lightman. 'I didn't know you were the Chester's solicitor.'

'What business is that of yours?' he answered.

'Well… I,' the detective stammered.

'None, is it? Now, let's get on with what we're here for, shall we?'

Wow, Mr Mercier is good! I thought. My knee bounced under the table, fuelled by the passion Mr Mercier seemed to exude.

'Yes… yes, of course.' Lightman moved to switch on the tape recorder that had been placed on the desk, when Mr Mercier interrupted his action by putting his hand up.

'Why are you attempting to record this? I thought we were here for a statement, not an interview,' he asked.

'It is, but…'

'But nothing. I hope you haven't asked my client to attend under false pretences?' he asked, tapping his brown brogues on the floor.

'Well, no…'

'Good. So, it remains off,' he told them.

'We do have some further questions to ask and depending on the answers we may consider further action against John-Michael,' offered Detective Green.

Mercier scoffed. 'We'll see about that. It remains off.' He indicated back to the recorder. 'Get on with the statement, detectives.'

'Yes, Mr Mercier,' they replied in unison.

There was a knock at the door, and WPC Thompson brought in a tray of drinks.

'Hope you've put two lumps in mine,' said Green.

'Yeah, I wouldn't mind a couple of those lumps, never mind sugar lumps, aye, sweetheart,' said Lightman. He made a clicking sound with his tongue and tapped her backside.

I was embarrassed by his action, but WPC seemed to ignore the violation.

Before she left, I quickly peered at her reflection in the mirror, and she winked at me. I knew it wasn't the time to smile, so I forced it down and held it in my mind to see me through the rest of the interview.

We had to go over the statement three times before Mr Mercier was happy with it. The detectives became exasperated with him, but I was glad to have him here handling all the difficult questions. Once the statement was completed, they had more questions for me. They took their time with phrasing each one to prevent Mr Mercier from interrupting them endlessly.

'John-Michael… This "Suit" gentleman that you've told us about… We've been unable to locate him, and we've been unable to find a single person who remembers seeing the man fitting your description,' said Detective Green.

'And?' asked Mr Mercier. 'Where are you going with this, detective? Surely you aren't going to blame my client for your ineptitude in being unable to locate the suspect. Now, do you have a question, or not?'

'Yes, I do,' Green snapped. 'I think John-Michael made it all up, and this "*Suit*,"' he said, using air quotes, 'is a figment of his imagination. A made-up story to cover his tracks. Everyone knows he's not right in the head.'

I chewed on the inside of my cheek at his words.

'To start with, you haven't asked a question, and secondly, are you a psychologist, detective? Have you studied this exemplary man's family background, his childhood, his school years, his conduct at work?'

'Well… no—'

'Then I'll kindly invite you not to *slander* my client. I can see your incompetence in finding the suspect has led you to clutch at straws. Now, do you have a murder weapon?'

'No, but we've an idea of the weapon used.'

'And? Do you suspect my client to be in possession of said weapon?'

'It's unlikely. You'll be hard-pressed to find one around here,' he said, sitting back.

'But not impossible,' added Detective Lightman.

'I highly doubt my client has been hunting down a rare weapon to murder his employer. Come on, detectives, you'll have to do better than that. Mr Chester here is an upstanding citizen with no record and a stable job for the past few years. What else do you have? Because that will never stick with the CPS.' Now he sat back in his chair. I could see him smiling in the mirror.

'He has a motive,' said Green.

Mr Mercier chuckled. 'Go on, then, convince me of said motive.'

'Mr Chester stood to inherit the shop and the flat above. Is that enough motive for you?'

'Oh, nice work, detectives.' He clapped his hands slowly. 'I'd get that tossed out in thirty seconds flat. Mr Chester was unaware of the inheritance he was to receive upon Mr Phillips's death. It was written into the will that he should receive notification of the inheritance upon his thirtieth birthday and not a moment earlier, should Mr Phillips still be living. Also, I can get statements from both witnesses to the will within the hour, should you need them. I do believe one of the witnesses is a colleague of yours.'

Both detectives blew their cheeks out.

'I think that'll be it for now,' said Green.

'Great! If you have any more questions for my client, I suggest you call my office. I know you have my number somewhere, but here's another card for you.' Mercier retrieved a card from his inside pocket and slid it with one finger over to the detectives, then he ushered me out of the room to where Mum was waiting for us.

'How did it go?' she asked, standing up.

'As expected, there's nothing to worry about, Mrs Chester. I'm taking care of everything.'

'Thank you, Mr Mercier. I'm glad we've got you on my boy's side.' Her body turned to me. 'Say thank you to the man,' she said.

'Thank you, Mr Mercier.'

He held out his hand for me to shake. I stared at it for a moment. No one had ever wanted to shake my hand before. Not even at Dad's funeral. Everyone had shaken Grandad's hand, but not mine. I wouldn't have wanted to then, anyway, but still.

Mum cleared her throat pulling me back from my memory.

I shook his hand and offered my thanks again.

'Right, let's get you home,' she said, and we made our way out with Mr Mercier trailing behind us.

'Actually, Mum, I really should check on the shop. Make sure everything is okay.'

'Oh, good idea. I'll join you.'

I stopped in my tracks, twiddling my hands in front of me. 'If you don't mind, Mum, I'd rather go on my own... I need a minute to myself.'

She stopped, too, and turned around. 'Oh.' She sounded disappointed with the way her tone sloped downwards. 'Sure thing. I'll... umm... just head home, then.'

'I'll drop you off, Mrs Chester,' Mr Mercier said from behind me.

'Thanks, that's truly kind of you. Alright John-Michael, off you trot.'

I watched them disappear to Mr Mercier's car before embarking down the pavement, towards the antique shop. I had a plan to retrieve the guns from the safe and get them home without incident.

As I walked there, I thought about the weeks leading up to Mr Phillips's death. I blamed myself. It was obvious now he had been in trouble, and he had let on something terrible was going to happen. I wished I'd had the nuance at the time to fit all the pieces together instead of being consumed by the search for *my* missing puzzle piece.

I weaved up and down the side streets and alleyways in an attempt to avoid the townsfolk. It may have taken me longer to get there, but at least I could avoid being seen. To return home, I would need to use the tiny alley between the hardware store and greengrocers, and I'd have to be extra careful. Since Mr Phillips's death, news had spread fast, and I was their number one suspect, regardless of the police's attempts to find out more about the true killer.

I managed to get to the back of the shop without incident and took the case containing the guns from the safe. I searched the shop for something to carry it in and found an old army khaki canvass shoulder bag. I fastened the buckles as tight as they would go and put the bag across my body.

I held on to it tightly as I went back into the open. The interview had taken longer than I'd thought; the sun had started to set, but at least the wind had died down.

The early evening was quiet. Too quiet.

I rounded the back of the houses, behind the shops, then did a U-turn to exit via the alley near the chemist. I had to get onto the high street so I could cross over to the greengrocers.

I poked my head out and scanned the street.

My stomach dropped.

He was back. The Suit was back. Except he no longer wore a suit. He'd changed his clothes to a checked shirt which was tucked into a pair of jeans. Despite his disguise, I knew it was him; I'd never forget the face that haunted me. The face that danced in front of my own whenever I looked in the mirror.

I leant against the wall and held the bag tighter.

I'd hoped he'd gone back to wherever he'd come from. Surely The Suit had to be aware the police were looking for him. On the other hand, perhaps he didn't care. Maybe that's why he'd swapped his outfit.

What was I going to do? He was in my way and now the guns were out in the open.

I couldn't go back the other way. I'd be too near the police station. I'd be in the open for too long. If PC Williams spotted me, he might stop me and demand to know what I was carrying.

Then he would know I'd lied. Everyone would.

I checked again. The Suit was leant casually against the hardware shop, his knee tucked so his foot was touching the wall.

You can do this, John-Michael, I told myself. *Keep calm and stay cool.*

I needed a distraction. But what?

I stuck my head out again. A white transit van had pulled up at the greengrocers, blocking my view.

Crap! Now, what would I do? I'd have to go back to the shop and wait it out.

As I turned, a phrase Mum had said popped into my head: 'Why should we skulk off like wounded animals?'

She was right; I had to be brave. I was the Mirror Man. I'd spent years under the radar. Why would now be any different?

Two large men in suits jumped from the van, and I recognised them immediately. I'd seen them near The Suit shortly after Mr Phillips's death. Were they going to put me in the van, take me somewhere?

The Suit bowed his head and pulled deeper into the shadows.

I watched intently. They didn't so much as glance at him as they entered the greengrocers. The Suit was now like me: unassuming, invisible. They weren't with him at all. In fact, he seemed wary of them.

I knew then I could accomplish my mission. So I pulled the collar up on my jacket and got ready to run.

First, I needed a car to pass so I could run behind it and get to the transit van.

I poised, ready to run, almost bouncing on my heels.

An old Ford trundled along. I counted.

One.

Two.

Three.

Go.

I crouched as I ran and pressed the bag close to my body with my elbow.

I made it to the doors at the back of the van and exhaled the breath I'd been holding. I was one step closer to where I needed to be.

The van door slammed.

The engine spluttered to life.

Oh no! I had to move now, or face being stood in the street, unprotected.

It started to move.

I darted off, like a greyhound being released from the starting gate and didn't dare turn back, scared of what might be lurking behind me. I sprinted until stars danced in front of my eyes and I had to stop to get my breathing under control before continuing home.

CHAPTER TWENTY-TWO

IN THE DAYS LEADING up to Mr Phillips's funeral, I became a little obsessed with The Suit. I had to find out who he was, where he'd come from, and most of all, why no one else had seen him. Plus, I had to do something. The police investigation had ground to a halt, and I couldn't let Mr Phillips's killer go unpunished.

I would get into the same mindset as him and see if I could figure out all the answers to my questions. And that meant I had to become him. I was the Mirror Man, after all.

The first thing I did was go out and get a suit similar to his. There weren't any decent shops here. I had to travel to Doncaster on the bus to visit Ray Allen's. I bought myself an off-the-peg, two-tone suit in burgundy and another one in silvery-grey. When I'd described The Suit's outfit to the assistant, he told me the name was *two-tone*.

Mum didn't mind being in the antique shop on her own; she enjoyed working there. It was the first time she'd been employed and had a wage packet. She hoped to save up and go abroad one day, she told me.

I minded, though, so I had Grandad stay in the shop with her that day. The next day, however, I planned to get my hair cut to the same style as The Suit's. The town barber seemed to be the only person who wasn't bothered that the rest of the town suspected me of murder.

I left Mum in the shop, telling her I would be no more than ten minutes and that if she was concerned about anything to come get me.

As the barber finished up, I saw The Suit again through the reflection in the mirror in front of me. He was walking past the shopfront without a care in the world. I couldn't get my head around why no one else had spotted him before now. I mean, they had to have. He stuck out like a sore thumb before he changed his clothes. It made me wonder if he was invisible to everyone else, no matter what he was wearing.

I quickly paid, tossing the coins on the counter. Despite the way he made me feel, I had to take the chance to follow him. At last, I would be able to find out exactly who he was and where he'd been hiding. I'd tell the police, then this whole nightmare would be over.

My heart pounded. Anticipation ran through me. I caught up with him until I was only feet away. That's when I noticed he was carrying an object in his hand. It was long, slender, and curved at one end.

What the—

I stopped.

Mum. The shop.

Turning on my heel, I sprinted back to Claude's Antiques.

'Mum, are you alright?' I yelled as I clattered through the door.

'Of course, I am. You've only been gone ten minutes. You'll never guess what I've sold.'

'Wait,' I said dashing past her.

I approached the back door; it had been prised open.

The only place the intruder had been was the office in a failed attempt to break into the safes.

'Mum, didn't you hear anything?' I demanded to know as she appeared behind me.

'Well, no I was talking to this couple about—' She suddenly changed her tone. 'We need to go to the police.'

'They won't be interested, Mum, I'm a murderer in their eyes! Why do you think we've had hardly any walk-ins?'

'We all know that's not true, JC. And I've sold the extending table and chairs today. Anyway, that's not the point. You've done nothing wrong.' She paced up and down the shop floor, wringing her hands. 'What if it was this "Suit" fella trying to rob the place again?'

There was no 'What if.' I knew it was him.

'Even if it was, it seems as though he's too clever for them to catch,' I told her. 'He must be a professional.'

Mum growled and stopped pacing to cross her arms protectively over her chest.

'I'm off to change the locks.' I told her. 'Lock the front door and don't let anyone in.'

'Fine.'

As I worked, Mum lingered behind me, muttering to herself.

'Right. Hurry up. We're going down there—now.'

I straightened from the lock. 'Where?'

'The police station, JC. Come on, hurry.'

'Seriously?'

She raised an eyebrow at me in the reflection on the glass of the door. 'Yes, seriously.'

Mum marched all the way to the police station with me trailing behind, struggling to keep up. Anger radiated from her, and the police were about to be on the receiving end of it.

'I want to speak to Detective Green or Lightman—now,' she said to the officer manning the counter. Loitering slightly behind Mum, I watched their interaction via the window on a door behind the counter that seemingly led to an office.

'I'm sorry, Mrs…'

'Chester.'

'I'm sorry, Mrs Chester, but they're off duty.'

She slammed her hand on the counter. 'Off duty? Likely story. I want to speak to someone who's investigating Mr Phillips's murder.'

'Ah, the imaginary friend case?' The officer started laughing.

'What? He is not imaginary,' she said between clenched teeth. 'He's just broken into my boy's shop!'

He hummed. 'And what evidence do you have of this?'

'The back door was wide open.'

'Were you in the shop at the time?'

'Yes, I—'

'And did you *hear* or *see* the so-called burglar?'

Mum sputtered. 'What are you suggesting?'

'Answer my question, Mrs Chester.'

'I… Well, no, I didn't. But the man is smart, he—'

The officer raised a silencing hand in front of Mum's face. 'And was anything stolen?'

'No,' Mum growled. 'But—'

'Then *why*,' the officer interrupted, 'are you here?'

'We need protection from that maniac!'

'I'll get right on that, Mrs Chester.' The officer's chin dipped towards his newspaper which lay open in front of him. He picked up a pen and filled in a few squares on the day's crossword.

Mum's fists clenched at her sides. 'Oh, if you weren't a man in blue, I'd—'

'Do not finish that sentence, Mrs Chester…' the officer warned and dropped his pen. 'You and your son need to go home and stop wasting police time. You probably left the back door open yourselves and forgot, but you've allowed yourself to become deluded by the boy's stories.'

'Deluded?!' Mum spat, but the officer continued.

'*Good afternoon*, Mrs Chester.'

For a moment, Mum just silently seethed. 'You haven't heard the last of me,' she finally said, then turned back to me. 'Come on, son, let's go.'

We left to the sounds of chortling as the officer filled in another who'd shown up.

I'd been right. They weren't interested in the slightest. Mum was furious. She huffed and puffed all the way back to the shop.

CHAPTER TWENTY-THREE

THE DAY OF MR Phillips's funeral arrived; a day I'd been dreading.

I wanted to get out and clear my mind beforehand, so I went to sit on my favourite bench, not because I wanted to follow anyone, but because I'd always been happy when I sat there.

However, I wasn't going to find that happiness today as I noticed a figure sat there. I knew that bench was for anybody, and obviously other people used it—their names were written all over it—but I'd never had to share it with anyone else.

As I got closer, I noticed it was Tab Hunter, and my heart sank further. I didn't want to listen to his ramblings, and what if he spoke to me? What would I say? Would he accuse me of murder too?

I sat down as far away as I could from him on the small bench. His bike had been leant against the back. In front of him was a plastic bag. I couldn't see what was in it. He stank of cigarette smoke, and he was mumbling incoherently.

I looked at my watch and decided I would stay for five minutes. I didn't want to get up straight away, or he would know I was leaving because of him.

I'd missed most people going to work, and the street was more or less empty except for Tab Hunter and me. I leant back against the bench and heard him clear his throat. I ignored him, but he did it again, louder this time, as though he was trying to get my attention.

I hung my head and swiftly turned to my right to glance at him as quick as I could through my lashes.

'Ay-up, lad,' he said.

I looked to my left to see if he was talking to someone else, but there was no one there.

He chuckled. 'Yes, I'm talking to you, lad.'

'Oh, okay. Hi, mister...' I said, not really knowing what else to say and wondering if I should get up and leave now. I'd never seen him talk to anyone before.

'I've seen you about,' he said, then rustled about in his plastic bag. Next, he clicked a lighter. It seemed he had retrieved a tab end from his plastic bag. I had always wondered where he kept them. He must have had hundreds in there.

'You don't like looking at people, do you?' he asked me.

'No, not really,' I said. 'I haven't been able to look at people since...' I'd been able to look at The Suit, though that was through sheer force. Then I'd been able to look at Fred, but it had faded away after that awful day. '... since I was young. I don't mind looking at people through reflections, though' I told him. 'I'm trying to work on it.'

He hummed. 'I've noticed that, laddie. Now, you listen to me. Don't let anyone tell you what you've been doing or how you act is wrong, *do you hear me?*' He raised his voice at the end, making me flinch away from him. I'd never heard Tab Hunter string a full sentence together before.

I nodded my head vigorously, part out of fear and part out of wonderment. I carried on nodding until he spoke again.

'You just be who you want to be, lad. Ain't nobody else's beeswax—'specially them police.'

'Umm... yes, mister.'

I heard the bag rustle as he got up, retrieved his bike, and started his mumblings again.

'Well, I wonder…' I whispered under my breath. Grandad would never believe this when I told him. I wonder if he knew the man was Scottish.

⟫⟫⟫ ⟪⟪⟪

At the church, it was the first time our family would interact with the rest of the community properly since Mr Phillips's death, and I hoped they would still come despite everything. Grandad said that today, all that mattered was laying Mr Phillips to rest—nothing else. He hoped people would put their thoughts aside for an hour to pray for Mr Phillips.

As we all sat in the front pew, I tugged on Mum's jacket to get her attention as she scanned the church behind us.

'Mum, are you sure I should be here? I can easily slip out before the service starts.'

She tutted. 'No, you aren't leaving. You have every right to be here just as much as everyone else, alright?'

'Okay, if you're sure…'

The vicar gave a lovely speech, but there were a few hushed whispers behind our backs when he mentioned that Mr Phillips saw me as family. Mum put a stop to the chatter with one of her famous looks. After that, all was quiet until we walked back out into the churchyard.

'He's a murdering git!' yelled Mrs Kelly. 'He should never have been allowed to this funeral. He should be rotting in prison,' she spat.

Mum pushed me behind her as other members of the congregation muttered their agreement. 'If any one of ya's got anything to say about me or my boy, come and say it to my face!' she shouted.

'Mam, this isn't the time,' whispered Tina.

'I know that, love, but they started it,' she said so they could hear.

'He wants hanging,' a muffled male voice said.

'Right, that's enough!' Mum said, squaring up to the crowd. 'My boy is innocent, and I'll have anybody who says different.'

I heard a bustling behind me and looked to find PC Williams striding towards us.

'That's enough, Anna,' he said, taking her by the shoulders and guiding her back towards us. Grandad was shaking his head, but he had a hint of a smile on his face. 'There's a time and a place,' he added.

Mum shook his hands off her shoulders. 'I'm only sticking up for my lad.'

'We all know that, Anna, but you know how it is,' said the constable.

'No, I don't know. How about you explain it to me?'

PC Williams ignored her question and told us to get home before people started showing up for the wake. I doubted anyone would turn up, but a few people did. It seemed some of the community were starting to come around to the idea I wasn't Mr Phillips's killer.

When most of the people who had turned up started to leave, I got stuck into cleaning the pots. Pete had offered to help, but Tina wasn't feeling well, so I said I was happy to do it alone, so he could take her home. I was scrubbing one of Mum's best plates when something caught my eye outside. My insides dropped, as did the plate in my hands, which smashed as it hit another in the sink.

He was back in his suit, mingling with the mourners as they left. Had he been here the whole time? At the church too? No, he couldn't have been; I'd have sensed it. Whatever the case, The Suit had found our home.

'PC Williams! PC Williams!' I yelled over and over as I ran through the house.

Grandad grabbed me as I burst into the dining room. 'What is it, lad?'

'He's outside,' I said, my voice now barely above a whisper.

'Who's outside?' he asked.

'Yes, who's outside?' asked PC Williams as he entered the dining room, most likely from the bathroom.

'The Suit,' I told them.

With that, the two men took off to the kitchen.

'Be careful!' Mum yelled after them as she took me by the shoulders. 'Sit down, love, you look as white as the driven snow.'

'Do you think they'll catch him?' I asked her.

'I hope so, love, I really do,' she said. 'Then we can live our lives in peace.'

I paced up and down the dining room for what felt like hours as we waited for news on The Suit's capture. But twenty minutes later, the two men came back, out of breath, red in the face, and sweaty.

Mum stood to greet them. 'Well? Did you catch him?'

Both men looked at their feet. I knew that meant he'd got away.

'We… lost him,' said Grandad between raspy breaths.

'What do you mean you lost him? He's a full-grown man, not a set of keys,' said Mum.

'He was faster than us. He must be half our age, Anna,' said the constable.

Mum puffed her cheeks out. 'Where does that leave us?'

Grandad shrugged and shook his head.

'Can I use your phone? I need to ring this into the station,' PC Williams said.

'Go ahead,' said Mum. 'You need to sit yoursen down,' she said to Grandad.

'I think I will,' he said, still breathing funny.

'I've phoned this in,' PC Williams said ten minutes later as he returned from the kitchen. 'They're going to send a couple of patrol cars out to look for him. Are you sure it was him, John-Michael?'

'Yes, it was definitely him,' I told him.

'Is that all they're going to do, send a patrol car out? We all know that means they'll have a quick scout around and finish up at the Golden Cod for a cod fry and chips. What about us? What if he comes back?' Mum fretted.

'I'll stay in my car outside tonight, and we'll see what we can sort out tomorrow, alright?'

'I guess…' she said.

'I'll be outside if you need me,' PC Williams said, leaving the rest of us to wait in awkward silence.

Time ticked away slowly. My head ached, and I couldn't sit still for long. I switched between pacing the floor and sitting at the table, willing time to speed up and bring with it news of The Suit's arrest.

The phone rang, and the three of us jumped.

'I'll get it,' Grandad said.

We all followed him to the kitchen.

He turned to the wall as he spoke to our mystery caller. 'Chester residence.'

There was silence while we waited for whoever was on the other end to explain their reason for calling. Then Grandad finally replied; he sounded deflated.

'Oh… yes, thank you. I'll see to it. Goodnight.'

'Who was it?' asked Mum as he put the phone down.

'That was one of the patrol cars. They've not been able to track him down, and I have some bad news,' he said, rubbing the nape of his neck.

Mum snorted. 'What could be worse than a deranged killer running around town?'

'They went past the shop. One of the windows has been smashed,' he said.

'What?!' Mum and I chimed together.

Grandad only hummed.

'Blimey, someone needs to get down there. The place has probably been ransacked by now!' said Mum.

'I'm sure it's fine, Mum,' I said, though my stomach was doing somersaults, and not only because of the shop.

'Gimme a minute. I'll fetch some plywood from the garage and my tools. JC can help me board it up,' said Grandad.

'I'm not leaving Mum here on her own!' I said. 'What if he comes back?'

'PC Williams is right outside.'

Mum snorted again. I suspected she had no faith in PC Williams's protection.

'Okay...' I said reluctantly.

Mum sat down at the kitchen table.

'We'll get changed. JC, meet me in the car in ten. I'll load up the wood and tools.'

'Are you sure, Grandad? You don't look too well.' It was true; he'd been pale and out of breath since trying to chase down The Suit.

'I'm fine,' he snapped as he exited the room.

'Will you be okay while we're gone, Mum?' I asked her.

'Don't worry about me, lad, I can take care of myself. Just be as quick as you can, okay?'

I nodded and went to get changed. I checked the guns were still secure and then went to wait in the car. PC Williams was sat in his car reading a copy of the *News of the World*. He could hardly protect Mum with his head stuck in the paper. I leaned across to the driver's side and beeped on the horn. He stuck a thumb up at me and carried on reading.

Crap! I hoped he would pay attention once we were gone.

Grandad loaded up the boot and off we went.

'What was the beeping for?' he asked as we bumped down the uneven drive.

'PC Williams is sat reading the paper. He's meant to be keeping an eye out.'

'Don't worry, lad, he won't be coming back tonight. We chased him off good and proper.'

'Did you tell PC Williams about the shop?' I asked him.

'Yes, lad. Now stop fretting.'

I was worried, though. The Suit had got within feet of our home without me realising. He'd even followed me at some point. How could I have been so careless to draw him in so close? I'd played a dangerous game bringing the guns into our home, and now Mum was all alone.

All the way to the shop, I barely blinked as I kept an eye out for The Suit. I shivered as a feeling of dread hung in the air.

CHAPTER TWENTY-FOUR

AT THE SHOP, NOTHING had been taken, and I made Grandad fasten the plywood as quick as he could. I was almost bouncing on my heels waiting for him to get it done.

'Stop panicking,' he said. 'Your mum will be fine. PC Williams knows what he's doing.'

'Okay, but we really need to get back,' I said.

'Get a brush and sweep the glass up. Take your mind off it for a minute.'

I managed to get rid of all the glass. I didn't know what the window had been smashed with, but there was no evidence of it on the floor. Only the remnants of the window.

I kept glancing around, making sure we weren't being watched. I knew The Suit was responsible for this mess. But why would he bother breaking in again? He knew he couldn't get into the safes. Unless…

The pieces started to connect in my brain.

He'd been trying to draw me here on purpose.

'Oh no. Mum!' I gasped.

Grandad looked at me. 'What is it, son?'

I practically threw the broom back into the shop, not caring where it landed. 'We need to go home, Grandad—now!'

Grandad all too slowly put his hammer down. 'Calm down, lad, what's got you in a rush all of a sudden?'

'It was The Suit. He did this, Grandad. He did it to lure us here, and we left Mum alone!' I started pulling Grandad's tools back into his toolbox as I spoke, then closed it up and stood, heading back to the car. 'Come on!' I yelled.

With a dramatic sigh, Grandad propped the rest of the planks against the side of the shop, and joined me at the car.

We hurried back, despite Grandad's protests on breaking the speed limits, and when we pulled into our drive, I was relieved to find PC Williams had finished reading the paper. I jumped out of the car before it rolled to a stop and ran into the kitchen. The phone receiver was on the floor. I picked it up and hung it back in its cradle, thinking Grandad hadn't replaced it properly.

I paused and listened for voices, the TV, or Mum's record player. Nothing.

I was desperate to hear a sound. Anything to distract me from the feeling of dread I had inside my gut.

The same sensation hung in the air as I moved. I felt like a stranger in my own home. As though I was following the steps of someone who had been here only minutes before me. Their presence still lingered, casting shadows in my mirrors where there shouldn't be any.

I moved to the hall, where shards of glass covered the floor. *That*'s odd. I thought Mum was doing better. Why had she smashed one of my mirrors?

I sniffed the air. A sour smell drew my attention. I couldn't put my finger on it. The food from the wake couldn't have gone off already, surely.

I shrugged and went back the way I'd come to get the sweeping brush and start cleaning up, all my senses on high alert.

I no longer trusted the mirrors. They taunted me, played tricks with my mind, cast shadows of an invisible presence.

When I heard a thud above my head, I glanced at the full-length mirror opposite the foot of the stairs, expecting to see Mum coming down.

But instead, I saw long, dark legs. A tailored jacket. A red tie.

The Suit looked across the landing at something before making his way down, and as he moved, so did I. I shoved the broom handle through the spindle of the staircase, causing him to trip. His arms and legs flapped about as he stumbled down the stairs before crashing into the mirror at the base and landing in a heap with the shattered glass. I pulled back the broom and noticed it had snapped.

Two sets of feet ran from the tiled kitchen floor, into the hallway. Despite the commotion, The Suit didn't move.

'What's going on?!' yelled PC Williams.

'I'm sorry, Grandad, I've snapped the sweeping brush. How are we going to clean this mess up now?' I mumbled, looking at the third pile of glass I'd seen that day.

'Never mind that,' he said as the duo pushed past me.

'You've got him, JC,' said PC Williams.

'What you waiting for?' shouted Grandad. 'Get your cuffs out, quick!'

'Oh crap, yeah.'

I watched as PC Williams fumbled for his handcuffs. He dropped them on the floor before finally holding them securely in his hand. On the ground, The Suit groaned.

Grandad threw his arm aside. 'For God's sake, hurry up, man.'

'Alright!' the constable yelled back as he fastened them on the intruder.

'Where's Anna?' asked Grandad.

'Mum?!' I'd been so distracted by the glass I hadn't found her.

I ran back down the hall to the front room, her room. No sign.

Next, the back sitting room. Nothing, only some leftover crockery I'd yet to clean away.

I headed for the dining room. A lamp had been knocked over, casting a shadow on the floor. I moved to stand it up, but it wasn't a shadow. It was Mum, unmoving, still dressed in her funeral attire.

I crouched beside her. A small pool of blood stained the carpet near her head.

'Mum,' I whispered as I placed my ear closer to her face. She was unconscious but breathing.

'Grandad! Grandad!' I yelled. 'Phone for an ambulance!'

I stroked her hair and waited. I refused to move from her side until the ambulance took her to the hospital. Grandad promised he'd drive me straight there once I'd spoken to the detectives who arrived in droves.

CHAPTER TWENTY-FIVE

MUM HAD TO STAY in hospital for a couple of nights after the incident, she drove the nurses and doctors crazy begging to be allowed out early. But after that, things started to go back to normal after The Suit's arrest, like Grandad and Mum promised they would.

I returned the guns to the safe in the shop until I could figure out what to do with them. We cleaned out Mr Phillips's flat, donated his clothes to charity, and brought any items of value down into the storage room and the shop to sell. Business picked up. Tina's belly was growing. Life couldn't be better.

One Sunday afternoon with everyone sat around the table waiting for dinner to be served, I asked the family to quiet down, as I had an announcement to make.

I lowered my head. I could feel them all staring at me in awe. I'd never given an announcement. Ever.

'Come on, lad, don't keep us in suspense. What did you want to tell us?' said Grandad.

'Umm… what it is…' I chewed my lip.

'JC, just take your time and think your words through,' offered Tina.

I took a deep breath and let the words form in my mind before I let them spill out. 'I'm ready to try looking at you all again.'

My family gasped, then waited for my next move.

I looked at each of their faces individually, then they all exploded into cheers and rounds of applause.

'There you are, son,' said Mum. 'We've all missed seeing your beautiful baby blues.'

'Thanks, Mum,' I said, smiling at her.

'I can't believe it!' exclaimed Tina. 'It's a miracle. They really are beautiful.'

'Thanks, Tina.'

A warmth swelled inside me upon seeing all of their beaming faces. This was my family, and after everything we'd been through recently, I never wanted to let them out of my sight.

⟫⟫ ⟪⟪

The day after my revelation, I gave Mum the afternoon off to go shopping for some new outfits. I wanted to inspect the guns again to see if I could find a way of getting rid of them. I took out some of the paperwork and the guns, then sat at the counter on my wooden stool to go through it all meticulously. I removed the guns carefully, checking for any secret compartments, but after finding nothing of interest, I fastened it back up.

I was about halfway through Mr Phillips's paperwork when the bell above the door rang.

'Be with you in a minute,' I said, not looking up.

'Take your time,' a man's voice said. Then I heard the lock on the door being turned.

My head flashed up. Two large men were stood near the door. One of them turned the open sign to closed, then they stood sentry at either side with their arms crossed. They both glared at me, nostrils flaring in tandem. The men wore black suits, and one was holding a briefcase by his side. They were the men I'd initially thought were working with The Suit. A third man came towards me; he had the same tanned skin as The Suit.

I stood from the stool and stepped back from the counter, dropping the sheet of paper I had in my hand.

'Can I help you?' I said, trying to sound confident even though I was terrified.

'At last, we meet face to face. It's true what they say about you,' the man who approached the counter said, cocking his head. I detected a French accent similar to those on *Allo Allo!*

I had no idea who he was, but I played along, hoping what he wanted would become obvious.

'What do they say?' I asked.

'You dress ever so smartly. You have an intense stare and a presence about you. That's how my men knew it was you. Though I wasn't told you had blue eyes, they are... what is the word? Ahh, *exceptionnel,*' he said.

He was talking about The Suit. He thought I was The Suit!

'Everything they say is true,' I said, keeping up the pretence.

'I know we agreed three months for you to track them down, but my men have been following you, and they raised... umm... suspicions that you might be... ripping me off. You went missing, which is why I'm here. My men assumed you'd taken the guns and fled. But here you are. In this... establishment.' He said holding his arms out wide.

Things were becoming clearer. The Suit had been tasked with retrieving the guns, though I couldn't comprehend how this man, or his men had been following me, spying on me. How could I have not noticed a presence behind me? I was the man who followed people.

I was the Mirror Man.

Or perhaps I wasn't any more; I hadn't followed anyone for weeks.

Then it clicked. They hadn't been following me, had they? At least not the whole time. They'd been following The Suit, but then he changed his clothes.

'I would never do that,' I said, though he appeared not to hear me. The atmosphere in the shop turned thick and heavy.

'You see, I've been trying to track these guns down for a long time. They were my great-grandfather's. He had to sell them long ago, and every man in our family has tried to track them down and buy them back ever since. And it is me who has finally accomplished the mission.'

That wasn't entirely true, seeing as he'd sent someone else to do the job of tracking them down. But The Suit hadn't been trying to buy them; he was going to steal them. Perhaps he was going to rip the man off and take them for himself.

I nodded. I couldn't search my brain quick enough for something to say.

He placed his hands on the counter. He wore a big sovereign ring on the middle finger of his left hand with some sort of insignia on it. 'Is this them?' he asked, nodding towards the case.

'Yes,' I said.

'Can I check for myself?' he asked.

'Go ahead.' I stepped forward and spun the case round. I had no choice but to let him see. I was outnumbered and no doubt outsmarted. I guessed if the guns were important to him, he no doubt had men posted at the back door too.

'Magnificent,' he said, examining the inside of the case. He clicked his fingers, and the man holding the briefcase walked over and placed it on the counter. He copied my action and spun it around, so the case faced me. It required a combination to open it.

'Do you want to check it now or when I've gone?' the boss asked.

'I'll check it when you've gone,' I answered.

'Fine. It's in used notes, as you requested. Do you have paper and a pen?' he asked.

I retrieved a notebook and a pencil from under the counter and slipped them to him. He inspected the pencil like I'd handed him an alien object, then he wrote down a four-digit number and placed the pencil and paper on top of the case. He clicked his fingers again, and the other man walked over and collected the case containing the guns.

Then the three of them left.

I sat back on the stool and exhaled loudly. The atmosphere had lifted, and I pulled the case over and the piece of paper. My hands had started to shake as I moved the dials to unlock it. I pinched the clasp, heard it click, then carefully lifted it open—

And swiftly slammed it shut.

I got up and paced the room, then dashed over to the door and relocked it. The sign remained on closed. Back at the desk, I opened the case once more. There were piles and piles of five- and ten-pound notes—more money than I had ever seen in my life. A business card sat on top of the money. I picked it up and read:

'*Count De Molay, Vintner.*' On the back, a note was written in cursive ink. '*I'll be in touch should I need your services again.*'

With shaking hands, I took the briefcase to what was Mr Phillips's office and put it in the big safe.

I didn't know how much money was in the briefcase, but I knew there would be enough for a holiday abroad for Mum. Grandad wouldn't have to sell any more cars, and the bills for the shop would be covered for a long time. I could even buy Tina the pram she'd been looking at in the shop window of *Mothercare* in Doncaster.

I would be able to look after my family.

The End

ON THE OTHER SIDE OF ALIVE

Dead doesn't mean gone.

At least not for Caroline. Following her sudden death, she is given ten years as a spirit to wander amongst the living. While watching over her loved ones, she discovers her life with her husband wasn't as perfect as she thought, and her death might not have been a tragic accident. Delving deeper into her new existence to find the answers she needs, Caroline encounters mediums, poltergeists, lost souls, an endearing conspiracy theorist, and a mysterious spirit guide who offers cryptic clues to help her on a path only he seems to know. But can she trust any of them, or will the uncertainty surrounding her death doom her to re-enact it for eternity?

LOST AND LONELY: ON THE OTHER SIDE OF ALIVE PART 2

Destiny awaits.

Caroline has a destiny to fulfil—whether she likes it
or not, so Eisen says. The planets have aligned and
the clock is ticking. But not everybody is on board
with Eisen and Caroline's plans for the spirit realm;
the angels and other spiritual forces are in hot
pursuit as the unlikely duo flit from present to past,
from west to east, in search of the sacred emerald
they need to carry out the ritual. Can they stay one
step ahead, or will the lost souls be abandoned
forever?

THE LEXI LOAFER MYSTERIES
BOOK 1

Caroline's adventure isn't quite over as she joins up with Medium Lexi in the Lexi Loafer Mysteries coming March 2022.

ACKNOWLEDGMENTS

First of all thank you to our editor, Liz. We couldn't have done it without you.

Secondly, thank you to all our family and friends, who continue to support us.

Most of all thank you to our readers.

About the Author

Jacques Von Kat is the pen name of husband-and-wife writers Jack and Kat. They have been writing together for four years and On the Other Side of Alive is their debut novel, which was published in 2020. They are fascinated by the spiritual world, and it was at a spiritual reading where the duo first met. Jack likes to restore scooters in his spare time. Three of his custom scooters have graced the front covers of the best Scooter magazines in the UK. One was even used in the film: Faith filmed in 2005, where Jack was also an extra. They live in Northern Lincolnshire with their two Bernese Mountain Dogs and enjoy travelling the world.

Come and say hello on social media or check out our website.
https://twitter.com/JacquesVonKat1
https://www.facebook.com/JacquesVonKat
https://www.instagram.com/jacquesvonkat_author/
http://www.jacquesvonkat.com

Printed in Great Britain
by Amazon

68744104R00118